THE EXIT

Helen FitzGerald is the bestselling author of *Dead Lovely* (2007) and nine other adult and young adult thrillers, including *My Last Confession* (2009), *The Donor* (2011) and most recently *The Cry* (2013), which was longlisted for the Theakston's Old Peculier Crime Novel of the Year. Helen has worked as a criminal justice social worker for over ten years. She is one of thirteen children and grew up in Victoria, Australia. She now lives in Glasgow with her husband and two children.

Praise for *The Cry*:

'My hat is totally off to this writer.' Laura Lippman

'Brilliant . . . 300 pages of taut, sharp, chilling and often laugh out loud funny genius.' Lisa Jewell

'Astonishingly good . . . *The Cry* is a remarkable novel – its devastating power all the stronger for its realistic rendering. Brilliant stuff.' Doug Johnstone, *Independent on Sunday*

'A book you find yourself greedily gulping down.' *Herald*

'The harrowing plot keeps you gripped until the final, devastating revelation.' *Sunday Mirror*

'*The Cry* really is extraordinary. In a just universe, it will be Helen FitzGerald's *Gone Girl* moment. Read it at once.' Steve Mosby

'FitzGerald's punchy thriller fleshes out new circles of parental hell.' Emma Hagestadt, *Independent*

'Exceptional . . . this powerful noir tale is by turns devastating and uplifting.' Chris Ewan

'The way their world unravels is compelling and terrifyingly real. FitzGerald is a hugely underrated writer, but the initial success of *The Cry* looks set to put an end to that.' *Big Issue Books of the Year*

'It is not until the final pages and after twist upon twist that we are finally given a punch in the stomach, an ending that still leaves a question. Did she or didn't she? Is she mad or not? You've got to read this inventive domestic drama to find out. Highly recommended, read it and then all her others, particularly *The Donor*. She is very special.' lovereading.co.uk

'An incredible read. I couldn't put it down. A beautifully crafted, heartbreaking story.' Lisa O'Donnell

'*The Cry* is excellent; unsettling and filled with moral ambiguity. Go read her. Now.' Russel D. McLean

'This book takes a nightmare scenario and wrings every last drop of suspense out of it. It's gut wrenching in places, heart breaking in others, a purely visceral experience like very few other crime novels I can think of . . . 2013 has already proved to be a strong year for psychological fiction but *The Cry* is without question the best yet.' Eva Dolan

'Stunningly good.' Mark Edwards

'My favourite read of 2013 (so far – but I can't see it being beat).' Luca Veste

'I loved it. It's beautifully written and absolutely heartrending. I loved every page and couldn't put the bloody thing down.' James Carol

'What a book! Superb.' Michael Malone

The Exit

HELEN FITZGERALD

FABER & FABER

First published in 2015
by Faber & Faber Ltd
Bloomsbury House
74-77 Great Russell Street
London WC1B 3DA

Typeset by Faber & Faber Ltd.
Printed and bound by CPI Group (UK) Ltd, Croydon CR0 4YY

A CIP record for this book
is available from the British Library

ISBN 978-0-571-28789-5

2 4 6 8 10 9 7 5 3

For Serge

Four Weeks Prior to Death

CHAPTER ONE

I didn't get the job because I didn't look happy enough. The manager, a twenty-seven-year-old with a lingering acne problem, didn't admit that exactly. He said I lacked drive. When he asked me where I saw myself in five years, I couldn't say McDonald's. 'I'd love to live in Costa Rica for a while,' was my answer.

Mum called a meeting when I told her. It was to be held at 5.30 p.m., in the dining room. It would require an agenda. It would begin like the last one.

Mum (in that deep, serious voice of hers): 'Items for discussion: 1. Catherine's credit card bill. 2. Catherine's realistic plans for future career. 3. Catherine's sleeping pattern and housekeeping habits. 4. Catherine's future accommodation ... Is there anything you'd like to add before we begin?' – No pause before – 'Okay, 1 . . . .'

Screw that. I'd get a job before 5.30.

Mum had been pushing me to try for the only job that required fewer skills than crew member at McDonald's: care assistant at a place called Dear Green Care Home. She knew someone who knew someone, she said, and gave me a number to call. All I had to be was human, ready to start immediately, and in Clydebank for an interview at 3.30.

The taxi (5. Catherine's spending) dropped me off at the high iron gates of a spooky stone mansion. I almost expected an elderly butler to answer the nine-foot-high door. Instead: Marcus Baird, thirty years old at most, and owner of this establishment. He sat me down in the office at the front and talked mostly about himself. There were two mirrors in the room: a modern oval one opposite the desk he was sitting at, and a huge ornate number, frame painted orange, leaning against the wall to his right. He could not stop checking himself out in both. Was his fringe maintaining its erection? Tussle, tweak, aye, just so. Was he right to undo one button? Two? One, definitely. How'd he look with his legs crossed? Good, great even. He'd crawled straight out of a B-grade horror movie, this guy – the almost-gorgeous boyfriend who cheats on the blonde star and dies second (after the best friend he cheated with). The estate had been in the family for generations, he told me. His mother had transformed it into a caring and comfortable place for the old and the dying.

'It's beautiful.' I had my third-glass-of-vodka smile on. If we were at a bar, he'd be giving me his number and I'd be saying, 'It's not your number I need right now.'

'Have you had any experience with the elderly?'

'My mum's nearly fifty,' I said.

He hired me because I'm cute. I don't have a problem admitting I'm cute. I hate people who say 'Oh, I'm ugly', or 'I'm so fat', when they're clearly not. I'm slim and athletic. I have blonde hair, blue eyes, and I'm cute as a button, dammit. Ask the seven boyfriends I was with for less than six weeks; they'll agree. Don't ask the three I stayed with longer (never more than three months); they'll tell you I'm a vacuous narcissist.

Marcus handed me several pieces of paper to fill in before starting work the following day, and showed me my Disclosure Scotland certificate, which Mum had made me apply for two weeks earlier. Lucky I never got caught shoplifting during that pre-Christmas spree in East Kilbride, age twelve. He offered to show me around, but I said I was in a hurry. I didn't want to see old people unless someone was paying me for it. I didn't like them. They jumped the line to get on buses, they drove slowly, walked slowly, packed groceries slowly, paid for groceries slowly, infected us with their miserable faces, had trouble paying gas bills, told boring stories, smelt of wee, took up space. I was ageist, so shoot my firm optimistic face. I wasn't one of those young people who help old ladies cross roads. My mate Paul was. He even spent most of his spare time playing cards with his grandfather and taping him talking about the war (not sure which one). Not me, I avoided them as if being old was infectious. I don't think the elderly should mix with the young. They should be hidden. I guess that's what some of them were doing in Dear Green Care Home, only I was going to find them and would continue to do so for £6.19 an hour.

I was ten minutes late to the family meeting (6. Catherine's timekeeping) and was right to assume Mum would be furious. She sat at the end of the dining-room table with that I'm-very-disappointed look on her face. I took a seat at the other end and told her I got the job at the place she suggested and would therefore be able to pay off my credit card and maybe even gain the experience necessary to get into a postgrad in social work.

I wanted to do a postgrad in social work as much as I wanted to live in this godforsaken country for the rest of my life. But it was more pleasing to her than my last idea – to organise glam parties for extortionate fees – hence, the BA in Events Management at a college too embarrassing to name here. I can still see the mortification on her face when I told her I'd applied for the same course at three different underclass colleges. She almost fainted. Why hadn't I applied for anything else: Psychology, English, Law, Art, Environmental Studies, something – for God's sake, anything – that had meaning? 'You want to spend your career organising ice sculptures for obnoxious sweet-sixteens?'

'Ice sculptures are so nineties,' I eye-rolled.

She was trying to suppress the excitement now.

'Social work! What an excellent idea.' I could read her thoughts: *My Catherine might have integrity and depth after all!* Maybe I'd even climb the ranks to uber-do-goodery, as she had in Oxfam.

The meeting was terminated at 5.59 p.m.

'Got a job working with wrinklies,' I posted on Facebook.

Mary-Anne, Felicity, Greg, Hells, Frankie, Paul, Dante, Vannie and Rebecca liked this.

Gina commented: Eek haha :o

Craig (most recent conquest) commented: Hey! Congratulations!

He'd used two exclamation marks in one comment. He'd changed his profile picture to an obviously Photoshopped one that made him look like an over-exposed Tom Cruise when in real life he didn't even look like an under-exposed one. He'd changed his status to 'In a Relationship'. I un-friended him and headed out to celebrate.

Mum didn't like my friends. I think I chose them, and kept them, because of that. At school, I gravitated to the cool girls who wore too much make-up and sat at the cool-girl table in the lunch hall. They (we) started smoking and drinking at twelve, lost our collective virginities by fifteen (at the latest) and wore clothes only from Top Shop and only if they were pre-approved by Gina.

At college, I didn't have to gravitate to this type of friend. That's all there were.

Mum's friends were successful, serious, important and interesting (yawn). Her nights out and dinner parties involved loud discussions and knowing sniggers. They were rarely drunken, and there were never any stories to tell after.

Both of us had one exception. Mum's was Antonio, who grew up in the same street as her. They bitched about their children (yes, I heard, Mum: 'She's just so hedonistic! I'm worried she'll never be serious about anything'). Antonio would console her ('You think that's bad, John refused to go back to his mother's last weekend. Locked himself in the bathroom for three hours.') He'd left his wife because he finally realised he was gay, but never seemed to be able to get a boyfriend. I think Mum saved all her laughter for Antonio.

My exception was Paul, who I'd met in one of the mind-opening activities Mum forced on me as a kid. Drama, at the Citizens Theatre, that time. When we were younger, Paul was the geek I could tell anything but had to hide from my shallow friends. At college he was the cool medical student I talked about too much to my friends, but never introduced to them. His dad owned an abattoir, which I found fascinating and Paul found embarrassing and disgusting. He was eight when he first saw the dead pigs hanging from hooks in his dad's huge shed. He ran out screaming, cried for hours, and never ate meat again, which troubled his father no end. He was a serious boy, and my mother admired him so much that I wished I didn't like him as much as I did. Like Mum, he didn't approve of my friends, and taunted me about them constantly: 'You want to be a clueless mean girl, but it doesn't suit you.' Sometimes, he'd trick me into meaningful conversations (about the death penalty, for example) and say, 'Ha! See, you do care!' When my Higher Exam results (five As, but that doesn't mean Shakespeare and calculus are interesting, and that *E News!* and *Now!* aren't), he photocopied the certificate and framed it with a plaque at the bottom: 'Proof that Ms C. Mann is not the dickhead she claims to be.' He looked down on my college course and my friends. For some reason, he refused to look down on me.

I swithered about who to hang with to celebrate. Paul's for a drink? Nah, his exams were looming so he was out of commission for weeks. If he was taking a rare moment away from his studies, he'd probably make me play cards with him and his grandad, recently installed in a custom-built extension. Paul would be all chuffed, as if the job meant something, as if it was the first (inevitable) step towards maturity and mattering. Last thing I needed was a card-playing oldie and the patronising congratulations of his driven grandson. Tonight it would be Gina and Co.

They were as grossed out as I was by my new role. 'You'll have to wipe arses!' We were drunk by ten, dancing in a club by twelve, snogging strangers by one, home by four.

*

I arrived at work the next morning with a hangover and a lie. 'I'm sorry, the first two buses drove straight past!'

Marcus Baird hated damn buses but loved the hell out of me: 'You poor thing. The train's more reliable. Come on in!' He took me to the office and set about inducting me: bank details on file (his small leather jacket zipped, unzipped), application for first-aid training organised (fringe checked in oval mirror), size ten uniform of ugly black trousers, uglier apricot shirt, size six pumps and name badge handed over (double checked in large ornate mirror), my arm touched unnecessarily with a half-smile and an eye-twinkle. He'd probably try and do me on one of the two desks in this office within the week. While I was trying to figure out if I found him attractive or not, he went over the job description: To assist with personal care and daily living tasks; to maintain and promote dignity. 'This is a happy place, believe it or not, and that has so much to do with staff attitude. Any questions?'

I wanted to ask about lunch – Was there a Greggs

nearby? I could murder a steak-bake and a fudge dough-nut – then decided if I was going to ask anything it should be something that made me sound caring, so I said I didn't have any questions yet.

'Today I'd just like you to settle in. Take your time. The best thing might be to get to know Rose. Did you know there are many different types of dementia?'

I said I didn't. I didn't say I didn't care.

'Rose's is a cruel one – she gets stuck in a trauma that happened years ago, flits in and out of it. We need to take turns keeping an eye on her. Come, she's having breakfast. I'll introduce you.'

CHAPTER TWO

AGE 10

No one believes a ten-year-old.

No one believed Rose when she said she wasn't hungry or that someone was going to die. It made her so angry she spat at the farmer.

'Rose! Oh look what you've . . . I'm not the farmer, I'm Marcus,' someone who did not believe ten-year-olds said.

Rose didn't know anyone by the name of Marcus. The person hovering over the breakfast table was the farmer, and he'd made her furious.

'Don't worry about getting names right,' the farmer said. 'Eat your porridge.'

'I told you, I'm not hungry.' Rose pushed the plate to her left and folded her arms. 'How can I eat when Margie can't breathe? Why won't you listen to me? We need to get the doctor or she'll die!'

'This isn't Margie, it's Catherine. She's new. She's not going to die. Here, one mouthful.'

If anyone here bothered to look, they'd know that

Margie was seriously ill. Look at her! Grey as a Glasgow sky. There was no way she'd make it to the milking sheds. She'd inhaled the last of the Potter's Asthma Remedy at midnight and settled for a while, but had been gasping for air since three. 'Please, let me get the doctor. An injection is all she needs.'

'You've gone back in time again.' The farmer tapped his chest. 'What does this say?'

Rose studied the person. Around thirty, black hair, high cheekbones, tight grey shirt and tiny leather jacket zipped halfway, oddly dressed for here. He was still tapping at the name badge on his chest. 'Marcus Baird,' Rose read out loud.

'That's right, well done, I'm Marcus! And that's Catherine, she's new.'

She looked at the girl standing at the door: young, but not as young as Margie.

*

AGE 82

Dear oh dear, the thing had taken her back. Rose wasn't refusing to eat at the farm. She was in a place called Dear Green Care Home. She was an eighty-two-year-old. That's a whole lot of old.

And guess what?

13

No one believes an eighty-two-year-old either.

*

It had been three years since Natalie Holland had
knocked on Rose's door with an over-cheerful smile that
made Rose assume she was selling Jesus.

'Go away, please; I've decided against heaven. It
sounds tiresome.' Rose shut the door.

Natalie knocked again, then opened the letter box:
'My name's Natalie Holland, Rose. I'm a social worker.
See my badge?' She dangled her photo ID through the
slit. 'Mr Buckland next door phoned – he said he spoke
to you last night when you were heading off to Barrhead
Travel Agency? You planning a trip, Rose?'

'I'm considering Marrakech. Is that illegal?'

'No, but . . . Mr Buckland said . . .'

'Mr Buckland's a busybody.'

'He said you were in your pyjamas.'

'He's lying.'

'Oh?'

'Not that it's anyone's business, but I wear a onesie.'

'Okay, I've just come to check you're okay.'

'Why would you do that? I don't know you.'

'It's my job – Adult Services – to make sure you're
safe. I have banana and walnut loaf.'

Rose was starving. 'Did you make it?'

'No, it's from Peckham's.'

Nothing from Peckham's Deli had ever poisoned her, so Rose opened the door. 'I'll put the kettle on, but if you try and sell me anything, especially Jesus, I'll hit you over the head with it.'

And so the State stepped in, in the form of Natalie Holland. And while Rose detested Natalie's role – to investigate, assess, look after, take over – she couldn't help but like the woman, who looked young for forty-five (slim, edgy vintage clothes, editorial short black hair) at the same time as oozing the cuddly kindness of a sixty-plus aunty.

She'd done her research before arriving. 'Ooh, is that what I think it is?' Rose's latest manuscript was on the table. 'I'm a fan, huge fan.'

'I was about to go to the post office and send it to the publisher, actually. It's always scary sending one off, admitting it's finished, that you've done all you can.'

'Would you like me to read it before you do?'

As Rose made the tea, she readied herself for the usual praise (How did you think of that! So layered! So funny! Sweet! Sad! My favourite line is this, favourite drawing that . . .). Instead, when Natalie finished reading, she shook her head: 'I don't believe in bullshitting, Rose; this doesn't seem finished.'

'What?' Rose grabbed the manuscript and flicked through it. Last night when she finished it – or was it the night before? – she believed it to be her best work ever. 'Why?'

'Billy, who you sometimes call Willie and sometimes um, Brett, yeah Brett, he disappears halfway through, no explanation, just – poof! – gone. And some of the words seem made up. What's eravature?'

'Eravature?'

'You've used the word twice. Look. Is it a spelling mistake?' Natalie pointed to the word.

'Oh, eravature, no, no, that's how it's spelt.' (*Social workers!* Rose thought. *What kind of education do you need to be a bloody social worker?*)

'What does it mean?'

'It means, it's like when you. Eravature. It means to feel. Hang on, let me get my dictionary. Where is it? Eravature. Read that sentence out loud, will you? Put it in context.'

'It's not a word, Rose. And Tilly smokes? I don't think you're quite yourself. Look at the washing machine – why haven't you taken the clothes out of the basket before trying to put them in?'

Rose looked at the wicker basket, filled with clothes, which was shoved halfway in the washing-machine door. 'That is strange. Did I do that?'

'Who else would have? And last night when you were going to the travel agency, do you know what time it was? It was 2 a.m. Mr Buckland says you've been going out at night a lot, and leaving your front door open.' Natalie patted the manuscript. 'You're an amazing writer, but this doesn't read like you at all, so we have to find out what's up, because something is. I want to take you to the doctor.'

*

They went the following morning.

She knew what year it was. She knew the prime minister's name. She knew her husband was dead. She knew her eldest, Jane, was in London, and that Jane's only boy, Chris, lived just up the road in Gartmore. She knew her youngest, Elena, was in Canada with her partner, Mary. She knew her mews house was in Kelvindale. Ah, her glorious little house, bought with the advance from books five and six, tucked away in a cobblestoned West End lane, plants and flowers filling the tiny sun-trap of a courtyard. From the huge oak kitchen table, Rose could see into thirteen tenement windows, people eating and talking, coming and going; doing. Nothing pleased her more than people watching. She wrote almost all her books at that table. How she loved her house. She could never forget it. Yes, Doctor, it was in Kelvindale.

But counting down in sevens from 100 became tricky at 87, no 86, bugger it. And the lines she drew on the blank clock-face were obviously all wrong when Dr

Matthews pointed it out afterwards. She felt foolish and small.

Rose couldn't stop crying in the car. She could hardly hear Natalie, who was asking her something. 'What? I'm sorry.'

'Your grandson's still not answering. Do you have any other family here? I don't want you to be alone right now.'

She shook her head.

'Friends?'

'Barbara died last year. Stroke. Pamela five years ago, skin cancer. I never thought of myself as all alone, but there you go.'

'You're not.' Natalie put her hand on Rose's knee and let it rest there, which should have felt uncomfortably intimate, but didn't, and the next thing Rose knew they had parked in a suburban driveway. 'I'll make the tea this time, long as you promise not to tell my boss: crossing boundaries and all that bollocks.'

'I promise. But I'll forget I promised.'

Natalie laughed. 'I'll take my chances.'

*

After Natalie dropped Rose home later that night, she sat at her kitchen table and did something she hadn't done since she was seventeen. She drew reality, so she would remember it. She started doing this when she was ten, after Margie died, and stopped when she met Vernon. In each of the hundreds of pictures she drew – of Margie picking strawberries, Margie skipping to the sheds, Margie playing jacks and eating ice cream and hugging her doll – Rose included a pair of green wellies, often hidden somewhere in the background. The wellies were a kind of code. If they were in the picture, it meant Rose had actually been in the scene with her little sister, that she had witnessed it, in real life. At her kitchen table, she now drew Natalie's four boys eating dinner: Nathan, fifteen, Fraser, eleven, Leo, nine and Joey, three. She drew Natalie's surprisingly serious and suited husband, she drew pasta and salad and bread and wine. She drew her new friend; the warm-hearted Natalie. And in the corner of the kitchen, a pair of green wellies. If she looked at this picture at a later date, she'd remember that she knew this place, these people. The wellies were proof that she had been there.

Rose put the drawing in the chest with her childhood pictures of Margie. They'd never been published. Rose hadn't even shown them to Vernon. She sighed as she shut the lid.

Rose gave up on sleep after an hour or so, turned on the computer, and Googled the disease. 'It's like living in a maze,' someone wrote, 'and the exit is death.' Everything she read online was equally cheerful. She made a vow to look no further, and began to rewrite her shambolic attempt at a children's book.

*

For the next twelve months, Natalie worked hard to keep Rose at home. Alarms were fitted on windows and doors, meals were delivered each day at four. Action plans were written up, review meetings planned. Rainbows of pills were placed into pots. Notes appeared wherever she looked: Have you turned this off? Make sure you shut this. Your kettle is gone – the home help will bring tea. Activities were planned, and abandoned. 'I will not get in that van! Won't sit in that circle! Where is Natalie? Get Natalie.'

Natalie did things she wasn't supposed to do, and she didn't hide this fact from Rose. She advised her to start withdrawing money from her account, and when Rose understood and agreed, she suggested places she could hide it. 'You might need this money, Rose, for clothes or music or books or something,' Natalie said as they sealed envelopes containing £1,000 each and slid them inside the covers of Tilly books. 'Keep it safe. If you move somewhere else, take these books with you and hide the envelopes somewhere in your room.'

Eventually, there was a review meeting in the Partick Social Work office. Rose's daughter Jane came all the way from London to attend, spending half her time yelling 'sell' to someone on her mobile phone and the other half complaining about the incompetence of social workers and the outright failure of 'care in the community'. Her grandson, Chris, was also present, as well as Natalie, and Natalie's cocky young male boss, and a woman who took notes, and a man who also took notes. It was decided that Rose's beautiful mews home would be sold in order to buy her some time in a home.

Natalie cooked Rose a special meal after that meeting, and the boys each gave her a present (pencils, pens, a sketch pad, two dozen stamped envelopes with Natalie's name and address written on them). Later, back in her own house, Rose gave Natalie a present: the chest full of childhood drawings, and the ones she'd drawn this last year. She explained about the wellie boots in each picture. 'You can throw them out if you want, they're not worth anything, just diaries really.'

'I won't ever throw them out,' Natalie said. 'And I'll visit you. I'll visit you too much.'

*

It was Chris who suggested Dear Green Care Home as it was very pretty, not too far from his house, and had excellent inspection reports. He drove her there on a sunny Saturday. 'Look at that gorgeous building! All rooms are en suite and yours has a view of the rose garden. Isn't that perfect, a rose garden for Rose?'

It certainly was beautiful. Like a castle, giving her princess-vibes. 'We should stay an extra night and go for dinner at the old Ginn House!' She could imagine staying here two nights, no more. While Rose loved nature, it was hustle and bustle she enjoyed most, and there was none of that here, just gardens, fields, a river. If she couldn't watch people, like she did from the kitchen table of her mews house, like she did when she sauntered around the West End of Glasgow, ambling through unknown routes, chatting to shop owners and dog walkers as she did, she'd probably shrivel up and die.

'It's a care home, Gran. There are people here who'll cook for you.'

'Ah . . .' She'd noticed the ramp leading to the front door and an ambulance parked beside it. A trolley was being wheeled out the wide front door with a sheet-covered body on it. She remembered where she was. There'd be no more weekend breaks for Rose, no more heading off to the airport with a small backpack filled with one change of clothes and drawing materials, no more dinners at fabulous restaurants by herself. She loved eating out by herself. This Rose was gone, this Rose had reached the exit to the maze.

*

It was group activity time at Dear Green and Marcus, a wannabe novelist himself, had brought in a local author especially for Rose. H. R. Davids, writer of detective fiction. Rose didn't like women who made themselves genderless (no, male) to sell more. She didn't want to call her 'H' or 'HR'. What the fuck was her name?

Yes, eighty-two-year-olds swear. They also eat, and drink, and shit. They like some people, hate others, and have thoughts that might be described as conflicting and/or bad.

She was having bad thoughts now – composing a one-star review in her head that she could post on Amazon later. 'H. R. Davids will appeal to those whose thoughts cannot be provoked.' (Yes, eighty-two-year-olds know how to use computers.)

'So you were an author?' H. R. Davids had a patronising smile that Rose wanted to punch.

She decided to call the boring bitch Henrietta Ruth. 'No, Henrietta Ruth, I am an author, and an illustrator. Children's books.'

Henrietta Ruth obviously decided to let the doddery old fool's name-mistake go. A pitying frown, like a pat on the head, travelled from her thin lips over to Rose's armchair.

There were four others in the group activity room. Henrietta Ruth read for twenty minutes, each second duller than the last. A baddy. A body. A detective inspector with a dark past, blah, blah, blah.

'Well!' Marcus clapped when the reading finally came to an end. 'Incredible! Would anyone like to ask our bestselling author a question?'

Rose looked at the four other residents in the room. There was Jim, a sixty-eight-year-old ex-rock guitarist with gorgeous long hair and good legs, which Rose fancied touching. Jim wasn't old or frail enough to be here, and it had always seemed odd to Rose that he was. He did not appear to have a burning question. He was sitting in his chair, tapping away at his mobile phone. There was Nancy, catatonic. Beside her was her loyal husband, Gavin, who'd moved in when she did, even though there was nothing wrong with him at all (apart from an increasingly debilitating depression caused by being imprisoned in here with a wife who'd said nothing for four years). He shook his head. His questions were too big for an author of detective fiction. And there was Emma, too busy singing to ask anything – one line, on repeat – bonnie, bonnie banks of Loch Lomond; bonnie, bonnie banks of Loch Lomond; bonnie, bonnie banks of Loch Lomond. Her dementia was a kind one, though her incessant singing drove everyone else nuts, including Henrietta Ruth, who'd had to read on as the line replayed.

*

Rose put up her hand. 'Yes, sir, I want to know why you won't get the doctor for my sister. I can't understand it at all.'

'We don't need to get the doctor, Rose,' the farmer said.

'I realise you may not know much about asthma, but please listen to me, because I do.'

'Let's get you back to your room. Let's not get anxious. There's nothing to worry about.' The farmer held out his hands to haul Rose from the armchair. 'Shh, there we go. We'll go find Catherine. Remember Catherine?'

'But Margie could die!'

*

Margie was seven years old, with soft yellow hair and deep brown eyes. She was soft and pudgy and still inclined to choose happiness. They'd been there a month. Four weeks since their mum had waved them off at King's Cross Station to be taken to the country because bombs don't get dropped there. Rose and Margie had never been on a train, and had never been to the countryside. Their mother had kissed them matter-of-factly at the station in order to reassure them, she supposed, that this was nothing major. As soon as they got in the carriage, her mother turned and left. Maybe she cried as she walked away. She'd be alone in London now. Alone in the one bedroom tenement they called home. Rose watched until she disappeared. Bye, Mum.

The train was a fast, rattling machine, cram-packed with children of all ages, many of them sobbing. Rose hugged Margie, who held her precious doll, Violet, into her chest the entire trip, stroked her hair, refused to cry because she was the grown-up now. She was in charge.

'Are we going to be okay Ro-Ro?' Margie had always called her Ro-Ro; she was the only person who did, and the only person Rose would ever allow.

'We're going to be perfect, angel.'

The farmer picked them up at the town hall in Penrith. He was a crooked man, leant to the left as he walked. Perhaps the crookedness had made him unhappy, or was it the other way round? As several men in raggedy, dirty country clothes entered the hall to claim their prizes, Rose prayed he would not be their farmer. Her hand squeezed Margie's too tightly as he walked towards them with his squinty back, his limping legs, his tight, mean eyes. He gestured with a hand – come now. They followed him, walking two miles in the rain until they reached their new home. During the train journey, Rose had imagined a grand country house with hedges and a rose garden. She'd dreamt of pretty lambs to feed and love, of cats and dogs and happy chubby farmy-type people. When they finally reached the small boggy ramshackle residence, Rose had to work very hard to hide her disappointment. There were no happy people here. The miserable monosyllabic farmer, his bedridden wife, and four other city children who had taken the farmer's lead and turned miserable and mute.

Once there, the farmer set about making them safe: make your bed, clean the floor, milk the cows, be quiet, you brazen hussies – whatever that meant – stir the soup, clean the kitchen, squeeze, squirt, cows, squirt, I said be quiet!

*

'Now, Rose,' the farmer said once she was back in her room, 'calm down, nice and quiet, there are no cows here. Catherine will put on your favourite tune.'

The music came from a very small machine on the bedside table.

'Imagination.' Yes, this was her favourite tune! Every night since they arrived here, Margie would say, 'Sing it, Ro-Ro; sing me the song.' Margie would drift off to her big sister's voice, imagining they were at home, and that everything was as it should be. But that machine was so small!

'And now I want you to sit at the desk and spend

some time going through your special things. Take your time, look at each object and talk to Catherine about them.'

Rose sat at her desk as the farmer ordered and reminded herself that she had to play ball in order to do what she was going to do. She rolled her eyes at Margie (not Catherine!), and then pretended to study the 'special' things on her desk. Photos of the faces of strangers. A bad drawing. Some children's books. Coloured pencils, lead writing pencils, a huge pile of the crispest whitest paper she'd ever seen. These things were not special to her. They weren't even hers. But she had to play ball, so she lifted the light orange pencil and began to draw.

*

AGE 82

She wasn't always aware of the transitions, but when Natalie used to visit she told her she drifted back to ten quite often. She wasn't drifting anywhere now, everything was clear. Coloured pencils. She had to draw!

Drawing was the only way now because they had taken everything else since Beatrice died. She wasn't allowed to leave the premises. Her mobile phone had been confiscated. The phone in the office: out of bounds.

Letter writing? Not permitted. (They even took the latest stash of stamped addressed envelopes Natalie had given her.) No visitors either, except Chris. She was not allowed to do anything but draw Tilly stories. All for her own good, of course. 'You nearly drowned last time you went for a walk,' Chris had told her. 'We can't waste police time again,' Marcus had told her. 'You get special treatment here, you know,' Chris had told her. 'I protect you, I keep you safe!'

She had to get it down, now, before the lucid up and left. This girl was fresh and shiny new. Forget drawing, Rose should just tell the girl. Perhaps she'd believe her. The police didn't, Chris didn't, her daughters didn't, even Natalie didn't. Please, please, little girl, I'm not crazy right now, listen to me, please. Believe me.

CHAPTER THREE

This old bird scared me with her incongruous clothes – jeans and Doc Marten boots, baggy tie-die T-shirt, short hair dyed blackcurrant. An eighty-two-year-old punk, and mad as a hatter.

She turned her attention away from the 'precious things' on her desk and towards me. 'If you promise to keep a secret I'll tell you something.'

'Um, okay.'

'You promise?'

I offered the old lady a pinky, but she didn't understand, so I withdrew it. 'I promise.'

'What?'

'I promise I won't tell.'

'Won't tell what?'

Ha! She'd already forgotten. I'd never known anyone really sick, or anyone really old. This sick old woman was as unknown and as ugly to me as a ferret. That's what this woman looked like! A ferret. All skinny and bony and yellow-white and crinkly and she might totally dig her teeth into my neck.

'You two getting on okay?' A nurse appeared at the

door. Her badge said Nurse Gabriella. She had pointy tits, a grey bob and bright red lipstick.

Rose looked terrified when she spotted her. 'You not heard of knocking? Get out of my room.'

Gabriella smiled at me. 'Don't worry. She just gets a little mixed up.'

As the nurse left, Rose turned to me: 'How do you know her?'

'I don't.'

'And the others? Are you friends with the others?'

'What others?'

'Out there, the others out there.' She pointed to her door. I assumed she meant everyone in the care home.

'No. I met Marcus yesterday, everyone else today. I'm new.'

'So you won't tell them what I'm about to say? You won't tell anyone till I decide what we should do?'

'Not a word.'

'Who do you love?'

'What?'

'Who do you love most in the world?'

'Um, my mum.'

'You swear on your mother's life?'

I crossed my heart, said: 'Hope to die.'

'Don't hope to die.'

'Okay, but I do promise, I won't tell anyone.'

The ferret lady leant in towards my neck, and

whispered: 'Something very bad is going on in this place.'

I took a step back. From the ferocious-ferret look on her face, I feared she'd be sucking blood from my neck any second.

'You're scared of me. Oh Jesus Christ. Don't be ridiculous. It's not me you should be scared of. You have to believe me! Are you hearing me?'

It was hard not to hear her – her whisper was becoming a yell.

'You don't believe me! I can see it in your eyes, you stupid little girl. Get out of my room!'

Nurse Gabriella had heard. She raced in, directed Rose to bed, popped a pill in her mouth, and watched until she'd closed her eyes. 'Stay with her, and don't let her upset you. She says the strangest things.'

'Okay.'

'And could you do a daily search of the room? She keeps stealing matches from the kitchen, always when she's travelled back in time. We never catch her, and we have no idea where she stashes them. She's fast and sneaky as a ten-year-old.' Having given her orders, the nurse headed for the door.

'But it's her room.' I thought I'd said this under my breath.

Nurse Gabriella walked back towards me and stood quite close. 'And?'

'And I don't feel right about it.'

'Oh, in that case, if you don't feel right about it.'

We stared each other out. I blinked first.

'Now do as you're told or go home.'

After Gabriella shut the door, Rose opened her eyes, looked straight at me, put her bony finger to her lips and said, 'Shh.' Then she closed her eyes again.

Scarier than Freddy Krueger, this woman.

I shut the door to avoid helping with lunch, and posted a photo of myself on Facebook titled 'working woman.' (Pose #1 chin down, fringe over eyes, serious expression, gorgeous obv.) Ten likes in fifteen minutes. Not bad. Craig hadn't emailed or texted about my unfriending. He would. They always did. And I'd ignore him like all the other desperados.

The bookshelf in the corner was filled with Tilly books. They were up there with Katie Morag in my childhood. Most families had at least one series. Obviously this old bird couldn't manage to read more than a kid's picture book. Mum had bought a box set for my seventh birthday and read one each night in bed. She loved how independent and strong Tilly was ('How a girl should be! Don't depend on some idiot to take care of you!'). I flicked through the one that was my favourite (Tilly and the telegram). So sad and uplifting still, this story. The farmer's two sons were at war. Bridget, one of the girls billeted to the farm, had collected the mail in the village, and it included a dreaded telegram. On the way back to the farm, she got into a mud fight with the annoying neighbour. She returned to the house covered in mud, and with no telegram. Tilly covered up for her, and dug through mud for hours before retrieving it. The farmer's oldest son was missing in action. As punishment, Tilly had to muck out the sheds, alone, until the war ended. But somehow, she found a way to enjoy it. It was better being in the sheds than in the house, Tilly decided.

*

Was I really reading children's books while a scary old alien lady slept in bed beside me? And when she woke, would she go on about 'bad things' again, or worse, need help going to the toilet? No, this was gross and wrong. I decided I'd see this shift out, head to the Queens for a drink, and work out what to tell Mum – something to do with health and safety, no doubt. The place was badly managed and dangerous! Did she want her only child to be seriously injured, maimed for life, emotionally damaged, for £6.19 an hour?

There were cards on Rose's wall from people who loved her enough to send cards, but not enough to let her stay in their houses.

Love you Granny Rosie!

Hey Mum, Sorry we can't come and see you, but you do understand it's for the best? It makes things worse. Gregor's been spending most weeks in Brussels so I've been holding the fort here. Work's going well, despite the economy. Got a new BMW yesterday – I love love love it! Hope Chris's looking after you, Janey.

Dear Granny, I wrote this story! Do you like it?

Dear Mum, Happy Christmas! Work and kids have been mad busy. Ally and Cat send their love. Big hugs, Elena.

There were black-and-white photos. A grim-looking groom, hers no doubt; dead now, I supposed. Two small girls in a garden. And there were colour photographs – the next generation, doing the same things as the last: getting married, having kids, smiling. She'd made those lives, yet here she was, alone, reliving a past trauma and imagining a present one.

If I wound up here, with the same cruel dementia, what trauma would I relive? The time Mum caught me looking at porn? Nah, that was just embarrassing. When Mark cheated on me? No, I'd done it first, and he was a wank. I realised I had no trauma to relive. My dementia, if and when it came, would be a kind bonnie, bonnie banks one. I took another photo of myself. Pose #2: fringe flicked back, lips saying Prune. Gorgeous obv.

And, at that moment, traumaless.

CHAPTER FOUR

AGE 82

The new girl, Catherine, was asleep on the high-tech chair that tilted this way and that. She was very pretty, but uninteresting. Rose studied her. No, there was nothing interesting about this young girl. If she included her in a story, she would be like Betty, thirteen years old, insecure hormones and determined self-love vying for control. Betty never did much in the books, except bug Tilly. She was a prop, static, something for the real characters to bounce off. The new girl sleeping on the chair even had perfect blonde hair like Betty, groomed for hours, no doubt, because her looks were her only asset. Rose had already written Betty. No need to write another, ever. No, this girl would never make the grade as a character interesting enough to be in one of her books. She looked like she'd been nowhere, done nothing. She looked like she had no ambition to go anywhere, or do anything.

Rose was looking at her latest Tilly drawing when the girl woke, but it wasn't making any sense. She handed it to the girl. 'What do you think?' While the colours were as vibrant as they were in all her books, there was something creepy about this one that bewildered Rose. Tilly was lying in bed in a room just like Rose's. A woman stood over her, with no facial features except for bright red lips. Four muted figures surrounded the bed, one of them in a chair. The text read:

> *Tilly did not like make-up and did not want to play Kings and Queens.*
>
> *'You're lucky, you get to be the Princess!' said the Queen, taking the lid off a fresh stick of lipstick. 'And a Princess is pretty, isn't that right?'*
>
> *'Very pretty.' The King smiled at his precious girl.*
>
> *'With beautiful red lips.' The Prince smiled as the Princess's lips were being painted. She was also his precious girl.*
>
> *'But not as red as mine!' Pleased with the makeover, the Queen twisted the lipstick back into its hidey hole. 'What a shame you can't press your lips together; kiss, kiss.'*

'I can't even remember drawing this. Can't make sense of it! Then, that was often the way with my books. I'd be three-quarters of the way through before I knew where Tilly would wind up.'

For the first time, an emotion other than boredom

dressed the girl's face. 'Tilly! Rose Price! You wrote the Tilly books!'

'You read them?' A fan! How she missed the queues of little girls at her signing table.

'Each and every one. Wow, Rose Price, of course! But this drawing is different, very dark.' The girl scrutinised the page. 'You gave Tilly a beauty spot. She doesn't have one, does she?'

Rose took the page and studied the picture. 'No she doesn't, that's odd.'

'And doesn't Tilly always wear the same outfit?'

The girl was right. Tilly always wore a dark green pinafore, a white blouse, and knee-length socks. And her red hair was always plaited in two. In this drawing she had short hair and wore a white nightgown with the letter B on it.

The room, just like Rose's. Beauty spot. Short hair. B.

Ah, this wasn't Tilly at all. 'It's Beatrice. Bea! She used to be in Room 5.' Rose examined the rest of the drawing. The door in the picture was ajar and you could see the words: Room 7 on its frame. 'I wonder why I have her in Room 7. Strange. I get the feeling it made sense when I drew it. Now, gobbledegook.'

'Bea died?'

'Six months ago. Alzheimer's like me. She was a dancer! Only seventy-one. So . . .' Rose took the page back from Catherine and placed it next to the one she was drawing. So far, she'd drawn Room 7 again. She stood. 'So . . .' She bent down and put her ear next to Catherine's mouth.

*

AGE 10

'. . . Your breathing's getting worse, Margie. Keep your head high. Higher than that! In slowly, and don't forget the out. Out!'

'I can breathe fine,' Margie said. She didn't look fine, though. All wrong.

Rose spotted the farmer outside the room, and whispered. 'We'll have to go over to the sheds again now. When he's not looking, we'll go to the doctor. Follow me. Come!'

*

'You're a selfish girl, Rose Price,' her father said the day before they waved him off at the station. She hadn't done her chores (that day she was supposed to sweep the floor and make the beds). She hadn't comforted her mother, who was to be left alone in London with two small children. He was usually a big old softy with his girls, so it shocked Rose when he said, 'You're a selfish girl, Rose Price.' Her dad had probably spoken to her after this. He might have said he loved her, that he believed she had qualities other than selfishness. He might have kissed her on the cheek, tickled her under the arms, called her precious and sweetheart and light of my life. But if he did, she couldn't remember.

'You're a selfish girl, Rose Price.' The last words she remembered him saying turned out to be the meanest words he ever spoke to her.

*

He was a storyteller, Rose's dad. Each night he had perched himself on the edge of the double mattress she shared with Margie in the kitchen alcove and made up a delightful tale that always had an excellent ending. He was far too talented to work in a factory. Too talented to be sent to war. He taught Rose everything she knew but the most enduring thing he taught her was that she was selfish.

Margie had nearly died twice before. At three, when the fever hit her harder than the rest of them and settled on her lungs. Her dad fetched the doctor in the middle of the night. Her mum burnt Potter's Asthma Remedy for hours after. Rose hadn't helped at all, but Margie made it to her fourth birthday.

And a year ago. Springtime brought it on. Rose

hadn't done anything to help then, either, but her parents got Margie to the hospital in time, and she made it to her seventh.

Squeaky breath, Margie called it. 'My breath's all squeaky.' Her face would go grey, she'd sit up straight and stiff, her back like a board, her tiny chest barely registering desperate cat-like inhalations. Last year, the sound was too awful for Rose to bear. She locked herself in the bathroom and drew pretty pictures of people who were not grey and could breathe untroubled.

Margie was grey now. She struggled to walk to the shed. Sixteen black Jerseys shuffled towards them from the south field. There was defiant Josie, sheepish Wendy, feisty Gee. Where was happy Noreen? Rose held her sister's hand, pulling her along. 'We'll wait till he's not looking, then run.'

Josie's wet-rubber udders were bursting to be emptied. Rose sat at her stool and began relieving her. Lovely Josie, the rebellious one of the bunch, straying from the line on the way to the shed, hurrying back to the field afterwards. Josie flicked her tail, blinding Rose for a moment. Rose rubbed her eye, checked on Margie, gasping for air as she squeezed weakly at Melina's teats. Where was the farmer? Nowhere to be seen.

Run!

*

The new girl was holding her arms too tight. Ow!

'Get off the road! Rose! A car!' The girl pulled Rose by the arms and they fell on the gravel at the side of the road together, the white van that had swerved to the wrong side tooting as it disappeared round the bend.

The girl was face down in the gravel. Rose had landed on top of her. Dear oh dear, she'd hurt her. She didn't mean to do that. 'What's your name again?'

The girl sat up, stunned. 'Catherine.'

'What on earth are we doing here, Catherine?'

CHAPTER FIVE

My mum gave me my first 'Sunday List' when I was five.

'These are the things I'd like you to try and do this week,' she said, handing it to me. I was starting at Hillhead Primary the following day – teaching me to read and write before I went to school must have been on one of the lists she made for herself.

1. Make three new friends at school and ask them if they'd like to come over to play some time.
2. Write a story for me.
3. Put your dirty clothes in the washing basket in the utility room. (This, Catherine, is something I would like you to do from now on.)
4. Make your own breakfast – cereal and milk. (This is also something I'd like you to do from now on.)
5. Do at least three kind things for others.

I got one of these lists every Sunday till I left school. If I did three of the five things on it, I received a very disappointing reward, like an extra half an hour of television the following Sunday.

When I got home from my first shift at Dear Green, there was a skip in the front yard, half filled already. I spotted an open box of old computer cables, faded curtains from the dining room, a broken mirror, the cabinet from the bathroom, some childhood toys, and about a dozen black bin bags. Inside the hall were some boxes labelled Oxfam. Mum was sitting at her desk in the study, writing. A list, in all probability.

I poked my head in. 'You work from home today?'

She covered what she was writing with her hand, and slid some envelopes under her elbow.

'Just this headache. How was your job?'

The boxes and the rubbish and the envelopes were all indicative of Manic Mum. Don't get me wrong, she was always manic – not in a diagnosable way – but busy, busier than anyone I've ever known. She never lay on the sofa. Never read a book unless she felt certain she'd learn something from it. Never watched television, apart from the *Channel 4 News* while she was cooking. She had mountains of energy and used it all efficiently. For sixty hours a week, she helped run one of the biggest charities in the UK. For forty-two, she slept soundly. For the other sixty-six, she made lists for herself and for me, and ensured that at least three-fifths of the tasks on them were completed satisfactorily. But by the look of things, today she was the kind of Manic Mum that only happened about once a year. She'd slowed a bit for the last two months and I was excited that perhaps middle age was calming her down. Or making her depressed, which was easier to be around than manic. But she didn't look relaxed or depressed now. She was at her desk, with that look in her eye that said: I've done everything I aimed to do today, Catherine, have you?

I was going to have sell the idea of never going back to Dear Green. 'I scraped my arm pulling a mad old lady off the road. She ran off so fast, you should have seen her go! It's not safe for me there. Look.'

Mum didn't respond to the bloody scrapes on my arm as I expected. (That's a shame, but if you start something, you must finish it.) Instead: 'How 'bout we open some red? Come, tell me about it.'

This was odd. We didn't have a 'glass-of-wine' kind of relationship. We'd never been drunk together, had a joint together, danced in the kitchen together. I never initiated a cuddle and when a sense of duty compelled her to, it was bony and man-like. She never told me she loved me and I never told her, not because we didn't, but because our respective roles – she the driven mother, I the rudderless daughter – did not require mush, or chats over a glass of wine.

She poured mine and sat on the sofa.

'So . . . Dear Green Care Home. I hear it's a beautiful old building. Tell me about it.'

I relayed the events of the day, my phone zzzing with

texts and Facebook messages that I wanted to read and usually would, but somehow felt I couldn't.

'And it's clean, and comfortable?'

I wish I'd lied and told her it was crawling with rats. I nodded.

'The staff – they're friendly?'

'I s'pose.'

She took a last sip, sighed, and attempted to stand, her left foot pointing inwards, a dead weight.

'You okay, Mum?'

'Yeah, yeah. Pins and needles, my foot went to sleep.'

She kissed my cheek and I blushed, like I did the first time a boy kissed me.

She settled back into the sofa and fiddled with the sapphire ring on her finger. Gran's engagement ring, it was. Mum hadn't taken it off since she died.

'Look, my finger's too fat for this now.' She pulled the ring off and smiled at it. 'Does it fit you?' She slid it on my reluctant finger as if we'd just said our vows. I didn't have the heart to tell her the ring was for fuddy duddies. 'Your gran was a conventional old bag,' she said, 'but God I loved her. I always thought she could have done so much more with her life, but she cherished Dad till he died; and us till she did. Now, I don't think you could hope to achieve more than that in a lifetime.'

I smiled at the ring just as she had. Actually, it looked beautiful on my finger.

'Cherish it, Cath. And defrost two lasagne, will you?'

A few days ago, Mum began cooking frantically, packing portions or home-made food into labelled Tupperware containers. The preparation of our weekly menu was always on her Sunday list (a list which always had more than five items, sometimes as many as fifty). But she'd been OCD for a bit, filling our regular freezer, and another that she'd bought and put in the hall cupboard. She had to do extra, she explained, because we were so busy now.

After planning my night on Facebook (drinks at Studio at eight with pals Gina and Co.), it was time for me to complete a duty from one of my eight-year-old lists.

At 6.30 every night, set the dinner table with tablecloth, napkins, cutlery and condiments which are appropriate to the meal listed on the weekly menu on the fridge. (This, Catherine, is something I would like you to do from now on.)

The conversation at dinner was always the same. Mum would ask me if I had any news. I'd say no. She'd say I must have and I'd say nah, not really, and she'd tell me hers, which was always about some famine or a political tyrant, and I'd always feel glad I hadn't told her about the fab new foundation I got on sale at Boots. Tonight she didn't start with the interrogation, just picked at her food in silence and didn't seem to notice when I left.

Marcus Baird called before I made it to Studio. 'Just wondering if you could come in tonight? We need cover from nine till two. Harriet can't make it in till two and Molly's sick. It'll be time and a half.'

I pondered the maths. If I worked there for a month, doing as much overtime as possible, I'd have enough for a ticket to Ibiza. I could get work in a bar there and spend all my spare time dancing on the beach. I could not be here. 'I'll be there in two hours.'

I arrived three vodka and Red Bulls later, mint in mouth to cover the smell. Marcus had his evening wear on – jeans, purple designer T-shirt and that leather biker's jacket he was always zipping and unzipping. He was ever so grateful. Nurse Gabriella was doing a double shift again. She'd show me the ropes, he said, and then he headed out to a gig at the Barrowlands.

Nurse Gabriella was like one of those women you see in a bank or in a baker's shop, the kind who is either un-happily single or married to a drunken violent brute, her only relief to torment underlings at work. She wanted to make me feel small. 'So, you've never worked as a carer? Hmm.' She wanted to make my life miserable. 'You can scrub the kitchen units. Then tidy the office.' She wanted to assert her power whenever possible. 'You're saying you already cleaned that? Clean it prop-erly.'

Being used to finishing things on lists, I completed all

the tasks diligently, but slowly, so she wouldn't give me any more jobs. It was midnight by the time I finished. I couldn't find her anywhere, so I closed the door to the office, hoping for some peace. There was nowhere comfortable to sit. Deliberate, I suppose, to stop staff falling asleep. I checked myself in both mirrors. (I needed to pluck my eyebrows and could maybe consider some leg toning exercises one day. Nah, they were fine. Were they? I lifted my trousers to knee-level and stood on my tippy toes – yeah, calf muscles were still there at least, thanks to my three-inch wedges probs, no need for drastic action.) Satisfied with myself, I sat at one of the two office chairs and started looking through the logbooks.

Note to self: If suffering from insomnia, read Dear Green logbooks.

They were in bullet-point form, mainly: medication changes, maintenance problems, messages from visitors, shift changes.

Nothing interesting in the current one, or the one before it.

I don't know why I kept looking, but I found myself going back through the months. Eighteen months ago, and earlier, the entries were far more entertaining. In between the usual shift changes and medical emergencies were entries about the people who'd died here.

Bill died at 3.35 a.m. He had wanted to die in bed, listening to Mozart's fifth, holding the hand of his daughter, Maisey.

He died in Room 4, sitting up in bed, listening to Bach, holding the hand of his daughter, Maisey.

His last words: 'Make this stop.'

His last breath: Gurgling exhalation, very loud.

He looked terrified.

There was no reflection in his eye.

And the one before that:

Brenda died tonight at 5.04 a.m.

She had wanted to die at home, window open, listening to the river, holding the hand of her beloved husband, Jack.

She died in Room 3, in bed, window closed. She was alone. (Jack died at home suddenly three days ago.)

She sat bolt upright and took a last silent breath. She looked excited, as if she could see someone at the end of the bed.

Her last words: 'You're there!'

At the moment of death, there was small rectangular shape reflected in her left eye (145.jpeg).

Jpeg? Why would anyone take a photo? Maybe the

relatives wanted one, or the funeral director required one, or perhaps it was just an innocent shot of something else altogether?

All the dull entries were signed – Harriet Gavern, Molly Wallace, etc. But under these weird death entries there was no signature. And the entries were all printed, with a fountain pen, judging by the frequent splotches. I skimmed through the entries before that. For over twelve months, every time someone died, the moment was meticulously recorded by an anonymous weirdo until eighteen months ago when Carmel Tate died (at 5.12 a.m. She'd wanted to die in her sleep, and she did.) No jpeg under her entry, just a weird code or something – zKgy48r9fP2_9b.

'What are you doing?'

Shite, Head Bitch had caught me.

'Nothing.'

'Well, we don't pay you to do nothing. Rose needs a change. Stay with her the rest of the shift. Do not spend any more time in here.'

A change. Holy mother, please make it a change of scene or a change of heart or change of playlist.

It wasn't what I feared – an oldie-nappy filled with number two. It was a complete change, top to toe. Rose had taken a shower, fully clothed.

She was ten again, thankfully, because ten-year-old Rose didn't want someone to take her pants off for her.

'I'll do it, Margie, you sit by the window. The fresh air might help!' As she took off her wet zebra onesie, she whispered frantically. 'I was swimming across the river, it's quicker that way. But then I don't know what happened!'

She managed to get into another onesie, a bunny rabbit this time. (Where'd this old dude get all her funky gear from?) She fell asleep a few minutes after hitting the pillow, and I was soon to follow.

*

When I woke, Rose had her hand over my mouth.

'Shh! I'm sorry, I didn't mean to scare you. I'm not going to hurt you. Just . . . listen.'

I was in the armchair by Rose's desk. The bedroom door was shut. Her art materials were strewn across the desk – she'd been drawing. What was the best response? Kick her? Scream? It was dark outside, but I saw headlights approaching. A car was coming up the drive. I gently prised two bony fingers apart and drew a breath, having decided not to provoke her.

'I know you think I'm crazy. Fine, that's fine. I am confused, most of the time. But not when I draw. The truth is in my drawings.'

She still had her hand over my mouth, so all I could do was nod. She sighed. My nod was not convincing.

'Do something for me. I'll give you this.' She had an open envelope in her other hand, with a roll of twenty-pound notes inside. 'Can I take my hand away? You won't yell?'

Another nod.

'You're no use, but Natalie will be. She knows me, and she's cluey, she'll see.'

There was a drawing in a plastic folder on her lap. 'Her address is on the envelope. Tell her what I said, about my drawings. What did I say about my drawings?'

'That the truth is in them.'

'Yes. Good. Tell her that. There's five hundred pounds. I see from the rota you're on late shift tomorrow. I'll give you the same again at two, as long as you've done what I asked. It's very important. You'll do it? Good. Tell her to study the page very carefully.' Rose looked out at the driveway. The car lights had gone out. The engine stopped. 'Go home now, Catherine. It's nearly two. It's not safe here.'

It sure wasn't. An elderly ferret had tried to suffocate me and was now scaring the bejesus out of me.

'And remember this, listen carefully: whatever you do, don't go in Room 7.'

*

There was £500 in the envelope. £500! And I'd get the

same again tomorrow. I said goodbye to Harriet, who'd taken over from Nurse Gabriella for the night. She was short and chubby, Harriet, with grey-white shoulder length hair that had mostly fallen out. At least sixty, I reckoned, jolly and kind, but with the most unfortunate facial features I'd ever seen. Tiny colourless piggy eyes, no eyelashes or eyebrows, a red lumpy, perhaps even cancerous, nose, and thin lips that couldn't close to cover her yellow teeth. Also, she smelt of cheese. I got a whiff as she saw me to the door with a 'Safe home and God bless'.

I smiled all the way home in the taxi, imagining a life dancing on a beach in Costa Rica rather than Ibiza, a life which could start tomorrow night. I'd wear nothing but a bikini all day. And tiny wee dresses at night. My skin would be brown. My legs SO toned from the dancing.

*

Mum was weird the next morning. She did her usual part for breakfast – making poached eggs and toast – but didn't pick me up on it when I arrived late to make the coffee and squeeze the orange juice.

'You look tired, Mum.'

'I was tired when I went to Paris, remember? I could hardly eat my ticket on.'

I laughed. 'What are you talking about?'

She laughed too. 'I really don't know.'

*

Natalie Holland had been making bruschetta for lunch, and offered me some when we got to her kitchen. She was around my mother's age. By now I realised that was not old. She was teeny tiny, about five foot two, and slim, with shiny black shortish hair that was wavy, but with a very short fringe. She wore a tight black wrap-around dress that forced you to check out her toned figure and perfect small boobs (wow) and she had nude wedges on that forced you to check out her legs (wow). Or maybe I'm just a perv. Whatever, this woman was cute and should be checked out and congratulated for it. She'd totally get it. Her house, a pebble-dashed semi-bungalow that I'd have labelled as depressing from the outside, was quite the opposite inside. It was messy in an organised, arty way, books and newspapers and magazines everywhere. Signs of hobbies littered the living room, kitchen, and garden. I noted seven – piano, karate, dress-making, drawing, football, Xbox, baking, guitar. This woman and her children – boys, by the looks – were into everything. They knew how to be happy. No wonder Rose liked her. She was still holding the plastic folder I'd given her at the door.

'So, Catherine, have you been working there long?'

'Just started.'

She placed Rose's folder on table beside the teapot, handed me a piece of tomato-topped ciabatta, poured me some tea.

'She said to say the truth is in her drawings.'

A sad sigh. 'Yeah.'

'What do you do, Natalie?'

'Now? I feed and ferry my boys. I was Rose's social worker.'

'Are you going to look at the drawing?'

Natalie didn't seem to want to, but did eventually. Her eyes seemed to well and for a moment I thought she might have understood something, that there was a message of some sort on the page. Natalie put it down on the table and sighed again. 'It's the same as usual.'

'She's sent you drawings before?'

'She started drawing this exact one about six months ago. At first, I wanted to understand it, to believe she had something to say. I thought maybe something bad was going on in there. When she moved in I visited a few times a week, but six months ago she started getting really distressed so I visited every day. I complained when her phone was taken away. They'd started treating her like a prisoner. I took her to the police station once when she begged me to – course, by the time we arrived she'd forgotten why she'd wanted to go. That was four months ago. The day after we went to the police, my boss hauled me in.'

'Why?'

'Ach, it's complicated. Someone complained. I wasn't behaving like a professional, apparently. I was upsetting her, making things worse.'

'So they sacked you?'

'No, I left. Might do some agency work, not sure. I thought after that I could visit Rose as a friend, but they banned me. I haven't seen her for four months. Now she only has Chris, her grandson. Her daughters don't even bother with her. Is she okay?'

*

I'd only known Rose for twenty-four hours, but I could already detect what year she was living in by the look on her face. She was purposeful but not frantic: eighty-two. She looked up from her desk, where she'd been drawing again: 'Did you get the page to Natalie?'

'She said to give you a hug.' I moved towards her, arms wide, not wanting to deliver said hug at all, but feeling it would be deceitful not to. Rose ended the awkwardness for me.

'A hug? Oh for fuck's sake.'

My arms slunk back torso-side. Phew.

Rose handed me the second envelope full of cash. 'Thanks for trying, Catherine.'

'I shouldn't really take your money. She didn't under-stand your drawing.' But my hand was already extending itself.

'Ach, surely you know by now I'm rich as a bastard. Take it. And if you're interested, I'd like you to try again. I'm not giving up.'

In my head, I was already buying a connecting flight from Costa Rica to Tahiti. 'I'm interested.'

'I'll finish a new drawing today.'

In two days, I'd have earned £1,500. I was beginning to love this job. I agreed to take the page as soon as my shift was over and felt clever and elated. There was something special about me. I'd walked into the shiteiest job in the universe; the one no fucker wanted to do; the one that required no skills, experience, qualifications, drive or vision, and yet . . . This was so postable, and Rose wouldn't object, wouldn't even understand. I changed the camera view so it was on me, pointed at my jubilant, wealthy, clever face, and began working on the caption in my head:

I am happy and rich and clever.

I just earned £1,500! Suck it peeps!

See me. See all you arses who thought I'd amount to nothing . . .

My posting was interrupted by Rose's voice: 'That's Emma.' She was looking out into the hall. Two men were carrying a stretcher with a sheet-covered body towards the front door. Rose's eyes followed the body, and she spoke to it: 'I'm so sorry, Emma. I tried.' Once it was out of sight, she wiped her tears with a tissue.

It seemed insensitive to wheel them out so publicly. 'Couldn't they take them out the back door?'

'It's too narrow,' Rose said. 'I like to wave them off. Will you come with me?'

We were now standing on the ramp at the front door. The trolley was already beside the ambulance. An elderly man and two middle-aged women sobbed as Emma was lifted and rolled into the back. Rose was still crying. 'Poor things. They missed it by hours.'

'Does it matter?' I wasn't meaning to sound cold-hearted, but it seemed odd for relatives to worry so much about being there the moment it happens. It's not like the person knows most of the time. People shouldn't feel guilty about it.

My comment angered Rose, who chastised me the way my mother sometimes did. 'It matters.'

I found myself responding with a snide: 'Why?'

Rose sighed. 'How old are you?'

'Twenty-three.'

'How do you want to die?'

'I don't.'

'You still think you won't, eh?'

'No.' But she was right. I wasn't even going to get old, let alone die.

'When the times comes, it'll matter to you where you are, who you're with. You'll have a last wish, and it should be granted.'

'What's yours, then?'

'My wish?'

'Yeah, what's your death wish, Rose?'

A dead arm fell out the side of the trolley and it made one of the grievers howl.

'I don't want to die in Room 7.'

Rose probably didn't have a good singing voice when she was young. Add old age to it and you had the thin wavering whimper that came out now: 'You take the high road and I'll take the low road.' I didn't want to join in, and wasn't the type to feel forced into rituals, but I was glad that I did, because the sound was less feeble with my voice in the mix. Behind us, a male voice joined ours. Marcus. And before we knew it, the husband and the middle-aged women in the drive were singing 'The Bonnie Banks of Loch Lomond' too, singing all the way through to the end of the song, by which time Emma and her dead arm were long gone.

*

When Rose was safely back in her room finishing off her picture, Marcus suggested this might be a good time for my first supervision session. I followed him round the back of the building and upstairs into his apartment, which took up the entire first floor of the mansion. There were hints of what the place would once have been – original oak flooring, huge central hall with open doors leading to several enormous rooms, narrow stairs going up to a probably creepy and definitely turreted attic, and a drawing room twice the size of most houses. But Marcus had stripped all he could of its old-world beauty, transforming his living quarters into a minimalist gadget-ridden bachelor pad. The wooden flooring, he'd painted white. He'd taken down picture rails, which had no doubt held portraits of generations of Bairds, and placed iPod docks and speakers on a wall in every room. In the drawing room, he'd bolted a television the size of a cinema screen where a fireplace should be. One work of exceptionally ugly art graced each room, two of which involved naked flesh and bulging eyes. The old library was now a box of handle-less black gloss kitchen units which opened with 'barely a whiff of your pinky'. All the appliances were hidden behind these shiny walls: the ice maker, the wine cooler, and the Italian espresso machine, which he was using now.

'Sugar?' Marcus sat at the polished concrete dining table and stirred sugar into our tiny cups of black coffee. 'What are you reading at the moment?'

'I'm not much of a reader.' The only books I'd managed to sit still long enough to finish were the ones on the school curriculum. I hoped he didn't want to talk books. I'd have nothing to say.

'Have you read *The Catcher in the Rye*?'

I couldn't believe it. I had, for school. It had bored me shitless. All that bollocksy male angst. If you're all so fucking alienated, then lock yourselves in your rooms and keep your thoughts to yourselves. 'I didn't like it much.'

He ran across the hall to his office, came back, book in hand. 'Perhaps you were too young. It changed my life. The way it deals with the complex issues of identity, belonging, connection and alienation: genius! I insist you read it again.'

I wouldn't read it again but I'd check Wikipedia for some dodgy but impressive facts so I could pretend I had.

'Have you seen a dead body before?'

I hadn't, I told him. I was five when Grandad died, and in Lanzarote when Nanna went.

He asked me how I felt about Emma as he washed our now empty coffee cups and magicked a door open that turned out to be the dishwasher.

Emma's arm had fallen from under the sheet when they lifted the trolley into the ambulance, a lump of flesh, disconnected, but that's all I'd seen of her. I told him I felt fine about it. I'd only seen her arm, after all, and while it was greyer than any other arm I'd ever seen, it hadn't scared me because I didn't know Emma and she was old and sick, so it wasn't a surprise, was it?

'It's five o'clock. Mind if I have a Prosecco?' He poured me a glass without asking if I wanted one. I put up my hand up as a No. 'I'm still on shift.'

'I'd like you take the rest off after what just happened. It's important to debrief. It can get to you.'

He had earrings, Marcus. I hadn't noticed that before. Tiny silver hoops.

'I remember my first time.' He was pouring us both another. He took a sip, waiting for me ask him to go on, which I didn't do. 'I was fifteen. Her name was Nadine. She had this amazing thick red hair. Wavy, not curly. Her skin was translucent. Y'know, the Irish type.'

He flared his nostrils a little. When un-flared, they were long thin slits, his nostrils. The flaring turned them into long fat ones that returned to their usual position very gradually. He had no nose hairs that I could see, probably shaved them with one of those special trimmers, which probably meant he shaved down there too.

'I spent my childhood in this place. Mum and Dad made me read stories to patients for pocket money on weekends and I hated it. Even ran away a few times. I found it scary – old people, dying. Then Nadine came. She was only nineteen – oh that hair! My first serious crush. She'd never said a word to me though her illness, but I believed I was in love. You know how it is. Anyway,

Mum thought it'd be good for me to be there when Nadine died, a kind of immunisation, to normalise it, so I wouldn't be scared any more. I was sitting by her bed when it happened. I remember the noise she made, the change in the colour of her skin, the transformation of her mouth and eyes from alive to not. I remember I could see the shape of her nipples through her nightie.'

I took another sip of my Prosecco: 'That's some weird shit, Marcus.'

He laughed and held his glass to mine. 'Hey, I was fifteen!'

Marcus's chinos were burnt orange. I noticed he had very round knees. I think there's something seriously icky about round knees, especially on a man. Earrings, fat knees, creepy stories: the points against him were stacking up. I decided to leave.

'If you really don't need me to stay on, I have something I need to do.'

*

Rose had finished her drawing by the time I arrived back in her room. She handed the envelope to me with shaky hands. 'Say the same thing. The truth is here.'

'What truth, Rose?'

'This is a terrible place. Bea and Emma died! Quick, take it.'

'Where? To Natalie? I'm not sure she'll understand this one either.'

Confusion descended on Rose's face as if it had suddenly gone out of focus. She repeated my words. 'I'm not sure she'll understand this one either.'

'Did you want me to take it to your grandson?'

'Chris, he's a good boy.'

'Are you sure?'

She lay on the bed – 'Of course I'm sure' – and closed her eyes.

I found Chris's address in Rose's file in the office and phoned for a taxi to Gartmore.

*

It cost forty pounds to get to Chris's house, a white-washed cottage in the one-street town. I was feeling embarrassed before he answered the door, knowing this mission was a pointless one, but he put me at ease as soon as I introduced myself. 'Ah, you're the new girl!'

Chris looked like the gay best friend I'd always wanted, but had never been cool enough to nab. My friend Rebecca managed to get a gay best friend when she was sixteen. Rebecca was horizontal-relaxed. Nothing fazed her. Nothing seemed to interest her. She only ever talked to me – in a slow, flat monotone – about other people's clothing at parties and clothing she had worn to parties and clothing she was planning to wear to parties. But she had something that made out-and-proud Frankie comfortable and they huddled together for years, talking (surely) about things other than clothing and parties. God, even Mum had a gay best friend. Why not me?

As soon as I saw Chris, I decided I'd get it right this time, and tried my best to ooze Rebecca. I relaxed my shoulders and put on the 'life's so fucking boring' face Rebecca always had. 'Your gran asked me to bring you a drawing.'

'Come away in. I've got a brew on.' Inside was as cute as out. Stuff everywhere, all pretty but nothing that seemed purposeless. An antique bread bin, for example, lid off, seedy German-looking bread inside. He closed the laptop lid on the wooden kitchen bench and poured me some tea. 'I feel terrible. I usually see her every day but I've been in Aberdeen. How is she? Is she all right? There's nothing wrong, is there?'

'No, no, she's fine. Well, I've only known her a couple of days, but I don't think anything's changed. She just wanted me to give you this drawing. She said to look at it carefully.'

He opened the envelope. As before, Tilly was in a bed in Room 7 and the woman with no facial features bar bright red lips was by her bed.

Chris read the text out loud.

"'I've had enough of this game!" said Tilly. "I'm tired of

it. *I told you, this is not how I want things to go.*"

"'*Oh, so full of woe,*" *said the Queen. "All right, all right, we'll have an intermission. Let's get the kettle on.*"

'She seems scared of Room 7, Chris.'

'Room 7 has damp problems. Not fit for the living.' Chris folded the picture, put it aside, and sipped his tea. 'After a resident dies, they put the corpse in there till the undertaker arrives.'

'Ah.' Well that made sense. 'Your poor gran, everything's so scary and mixed up. Oh, I promised I'd tell you that the truth is in her drawings.'

Chris's expression mirrored Natalie's after I said the same thing to her. They'd both probably heard it a hundred times before. 'Have you read the Tilly books?'

I nodded. The Tilly books were set in 1940. Tilly was ten. Her full name was Mathilda Greenthorn. She was an evacuee from London. She'd been placed in a country house in Staffordshire with some other children. She was always doing things she shouldn't and getting into trouble. She was always trying to help the other kids. 'They were my favourite books as a kid.'

'Mine too. It's so sad what's happening to her.' His mobile buzzed. 'Sorry, better get this. Work.'

He was talking to a cop or a lawyer, by the sounds. He mentioned a perpetrator and something about an iron key and an unknown male victim and a MAPPA score of 'very high'. 'Right, will do.' He hung up.

'Are you a police officer?' I had stopped myself using the word cop, and felt proud.

'No, I run my own IT business. The police use me as a consultant on internet cases.'

'Like fraud?'

'I wish. Sexual offenders. Someone's gotta do it. There's something for everyone online nowadays.'

Chris had been planning to visit at his usual time, seven, but decided to go immediately. He dropped me at the shops on the way, and I didn't manage to say a full sentence the entire trip. I know it's ridiculous, to be so in awe without knowing much about him other than that he was obviously gay. How did I know this? Just trust me. I'm not sure I have a gaydar, but even the gaydarless would know. I was star struck. He had a gorgeous stone cottage with the coolest interior I'd ever seen. His handsomeness was edgy and intriguing, a shaven, happier looking Johnny Depp, with juicy lips that'd be ace to kiss if he was up for kissing girls. He gave off a confident, kind, loveliness vibe. I had a fag crush. And I loved how much he admired his gran, mad old bird that she was.

*

I'm not sure I'd admired mine, but I loved her. She was a fifties housewife. She wore tight floral dresses. She

69

ironed underwear, sewed buttons, removed stains, baked cakes, made curtains. I guess it's no surprise that my mother rebelled against this. Everything her mum had done, she refused to do. Everything her mum hadn't done, she did with gusto. For example, my mum vetoed bras and skirts, wore jeans and men's shirts. She marched against Thatcher at medical school, she quit medical school, she lived with a guy who had a tattoo, got a tattoo, lived with a guy who had a drug problem, got a drug problem, studied international relations, got pregnant, married a guy she didn't love, and kicked him out a year later. She brought me up to be nothing like her mother, because women like her mother were dependent and weak and I would be an independent woman, she'd told me.

'But, Mummy, I'm only five!'

'And you are your own five-year-old,' she'd said.

At school that day, I wondered what being my own five-year-old meant. I still wonder.

*

Mum was crying in her bed when I got home. I heard the wailing sounds as soon as I opened the door, and resisted the temptation to go straight back out again. 'Mum, what's wrong?'

She rubbed her face against the pillow. 'Oh, nothing,

menopause! Sorry. How was your day?'

I'd already decided to keep Rose's money a secret. Mum'd probably tell me to give it back and I couldn't, having spent two hundred and thirty of it on beach clothes and make-up at Buchanan Galleries on the way home, and the rest of it in my head. 'Someone died.'

'Oh.' Mum's eyes welled up. In twenty-three years I'd never seen her cry (maybe 'cause I was in Tenerife when Gran died, but it wouldn't surprise me if she hadn't then either), and all of a sudden she was a crying machine. Funny, menopause was bringing out the woman in her, not the other way round. 'Who?'

'A woman called Emma. She sang all the time, that Loch Lomond song. She seemed fine yesterday. I saw her arm. It was grey.'

Mum just could not control her lower lip. I felt like grabbing it and holding on to it for her.

'Was Emma scared?'

'I didn't see her die. I'm sure she would have been. Who wouldn't?'

Mum put her face deep into the duck feather pillow, but not deep enough to muffle the sobs.

Menopause! I thought, heading to my room, putting earphones in to drown out Mum's crying, then trying on the first of three bikinis (red polka dot, halter-neck, this one). I'd rather die than be old enough for menopause.

CHAPTER SIX

AGE 82

Chris had come out to her first. He was seventeen, and happy as Larry about it, not tortured at all. Rose had hugged him and said she'd known since he was seven and was glad he was finally able to say it out loud. Only to you, he admitted. It would take him five years and a large bottle of whisky to tell his parents.

From the moment he was born he was her favourite thing in the world, even more than her own girls, who'd filled her with worry as they squealed their way into adulthood. Unlike them, he'd always been self-contained, hard working and happy. Beautiful boy. Right now, he was dying her hair blackcurrant. 'But it's already blackcurrant!'

'Your roots aren't, Gran.'

Once the timer went off, Chris rinsed her hair thoroughly, and gave her a shampoo and head massage that made her lose herself, bliss.

'What are the drawings all about? Is there something going on in that noggin of yours?'

He dried her hair and 'distressed' it with Fudge. He helped her into the new koala onesie he'd purchased in town that morning. Ta-da! He turned her towards the mirror. 'You look fabulous!'

Rose had to agree. 'I bloody do, don't I?'

'Now get into bed and tell me what those drawings are about.'

She was so comfortable, sleepy. Chris often made her feel calm. She closed her eyes.

'Gran, you told Catherine to show me a drawing. Why? You know you shouldn't be sending letters and things to people.'

'Catherine?'

'The new girl. You sent her to my house, remember? Blonde hair, pretty.'

'The dull one.'

'Yeah, her.'

Rose had no interest in her. She wanted to know about Chris's work. 'Tell me about one of your cases. What are you working on?'

'It's confidential.'

'I'll forget anyway.'

'Okay, I was monitoring this BDSM site: that's Body Discipline Sado-Masochism, and traced it to this bloke in Aberdeen. You would not believe the stuff that man was making.'

'Tell me.'

'No, it's too gross, honestly. Not the stuff of bedtime stories. Suffice to say his actors didn't seem too happy. He was producing as well as distributing videos.'

'Actors, producers, directors. You make it sound like Hollywood.'

'Well, it is a business. Folk make money.'

'Actor's the wrong word, though, no?'

'Words, words . . .'

'How do they make something like that happen?'

'What do you mean?'

'Well when you bought that shirt, for example, you bought it from a shop. The shop owner bought it from the wholesaler who bought it from the boss of the wee boy in China who made it.'

'Works the same.'

'No!'

'Aye. It's like this . . . The actor's connected to the producer, and the producer connects to the customers, when the customers connects to the internet.'

'BDSM, I must remember that.' Rose was drifting off.

'No, Gran, you don't need to remember that.'

She didn't know what he was saying. All she knew was that his voice made her smile. She felt him kiss her forehead.

*

She couldn't believe she'd fallen asleep. How could she have done that? Rose jumped out of bed and raced around the house looking for Margie. She wasn't inside, must be in the sheds. She ran across the wet lawn and there she was, standing at the fence looking towards the river.

Rose nudged Margie into the water, knowing she'd be too frightened to take the plunge, and waded in after her. If they could get across together, they'd get there in half the time. Holding her little sister's hand, she pulled and pulled until they were waist-deep.

'Rose, I said stop!' Margie said.

There wasn't time, but she had to take a second to convince her. She had to be responsible, caring. 'Okay, look at me, Margie, if we don't keep going you could die. Let me carry you if you can't walk. Jump up onto my back.'

'Rose, no. Let's just go back.'

'NO!' Rose let go of Margie's hand and pulled at her own mousy brown hair, screaming, 'Margaret Isabel Price, you must do as I say!'

Oh dear, the water was getting deeper, now up to Margie's straining chest. They were only a quarter of the way across, and it was probably quite a lot deeper in the middle. Rose grabbed her sister under the shoulders, hauled her back to the riverbank, and sat her against a tree. She gathered all the twigs and dry scrub she could find, and formed the sticks in a teepee over the scrub. 'Wait here, I'm just going to go and get matches. I'll be back in a minute.'

Rose raced as fast as she could back to the farmhouse, snuck in the back door, crept along the hall, into the empty kitchen, and searched for a box of matches. Where were they? Not above the stove, or in the utensil drawer, or under the sink. Ah, in the bread bin! When she got back to the tree, Margie's shivers had graduated to wild shudders. Her lips were turning blue. It took three matches to light the twigs. 'Stay by the flames. I'll be back soon. Margie, stop it, don't say that – "Hold my hand as I die!" What nonsense, you're not going to die! And that's because I'm going to fetch the doctor now. So you see I can't stay here with you. On Dad's life, I swear you won't be alone for long. I know, sing "Imagination" twenty times, and you won't be finished when I get back.' Rose started the song.

Once Margie had opened her mouth in an attempt to join in, Rose ran down to the riverbank and walked in, plunged forth when the water reached her thighs and began to swim to the other side.

*

They had a fancy word for what they were doing but in fact it was assault. Rose was tied to the bed. She screamed and attempted to kick, but she couldn't move beyond the plastic bands across her torso, arms and legs. Dull Girl was standing at the door, wet, and looking terrified, insipid idiot.

They'd called Chris. He barged past the dull girl and ordered them to untie his grandmother NOW. 'Get those off! For God's sake, she's Rose Price, not some criminal! I'm going to ring the police if you don't take those off her now!'

Nurse Gabriella unbuckled the bed restraints and Chris leant down and hugged her. Wee soul, no matter what, he was always there.

Bitch Nurse left after a few minutes, leaving Chris and the dull blonde one, Catherine, to calm her down by going through photo albums. Strategies, maybe, but they worked, and she welcomed them.

'Gran, maybe it'd help to talk about what happened when you were ten.' Chris had turned the page to a photo of Rose and Margie at the train station before they left for the farm. Margie was holding a small doll dressed in a pretty pink frock and tiny lace bootees. She looked on the shelf beside the Tilly books – the very same doll, Violet, was there. It was the only memento she had of Margie. And she had none of her parents now, either. Not even any photos, as she'd given the large chest filled with such things to Elena after Vernon died. Rose was moving to her mews house, and had very little room. She trusted Elena to look after them. Alas, Elena had emigrated to Canada, culling ruthlessly beforehand, and had given the chest and its contents to a charity shop somewhere in York. Elena apologised. She hadn't realised she'd left the photos in the chest. Rose forgave her, and tried not to be angry. But what she'd do to see her father's face. In it, perhaps she'd see kind eyes that told her stories at night, and not the eyes that said: 'You're a selfish girl, Rose Price.'

The doll was her most precious possession. So pretty, with a shiny little face and rosy cheeks. She took the doll from the shelf and settled into bed.

'Maybe it'd help to talk about it, Gran?' Her grandson was repeating himself. He did that a lot.

Rose nestled Violet into her shoulder, turned on her side, put her knees up to her chest. 'I want to be by my-self.'

CHAPTER SEVEN

I was taking a selfie by the river when Rose snuck up behind me and pushed me into the water. I don't know where her strength came from, but it took ages to get back out. I was too cold and shocked to move when she sat me against the tree, running off to steal matches from the kitchen. After they saw the smoke from the fire she'd lit, Nurse Gabriella and another young care assistant called Molly raced over, got her out of the river, and restrained her – well, that's what they called it. They pinned her down and carried her to her bed, and tied her there till Chris came. Although I'd earned more in three days than most of my mates would in a month, I was starting to realise this job was hard and stopped feeling guilty because I deserved it.

At least once a day, Rose relived a two-hour event from her childhood, Chris explained after Rose had fallen asleep. She'd run away from the farm with Margie to get medical help, tried to get her across the river, failed, left her by the tree, stolen matches from the farm's kitchen, lit a fire, left Margie, and swam across the river to get the doctor. Once in town, Rose had tossed a rock through the doctor's window because he wasn't answering the door. When they finally got back to the tree, Margie was dead. Run, river, matches, rock, dead. She didn't always relive the whole thing, didn't always start from the beginning, or go in order. Run, river, matches, rock, dead. Matches, river. Dead, run. Rock, river, dead, run, matches.

'The illness seems to make her fixate on the worst things that happened to her,' Chris said. 'Her dad telling her she was selfish, and Margie's death. If only it made her relive my mum's first steps, or getting her first book published – apparently she skipped all the way to the pub after her agent phoned!'

I spent the rest of the morning helping with tea and getting people to the activity room to watch some local pianist play badly for an hour while tubby Harriet danced badly in the middle of the room in order to encourage joy.

There were seven bedrooms altogether After lunch was cleared up. I decided to check them all out. At the very front of the house were two large bay-windowed rooms: the kitchen/dining room to the right, with a disabled toilet off the back of the dining room, and the office to the left. Behind those rooms were six bedrooms, three on either side. They varied in size, but all smelt and felt the same: a hospital bed on wheels in the centre, one landscape painting above the bed and one on the wall opposite, handrails and alarms everywhere.

They all had an en-suite bathroom with a seat in the shower and a raised toilet-seat frame with handles over the normal one. Rose's room, Room 1, was the first on the left behind the office. Opposite her: the catatonic woman, Nancy, and her depressed husband, Gavin. Jim the ex-rocker was in Room 3, behind Rose. Room 4, opposite Jim, had been Emma's, and was now empty. A twenty-one-year-old with leukaemia was in Room 5, behind Jim, but he'd gone home for a few days, so I hadn't met him yet. Room 6, which lacked an en suite, was used as a television room. And the activity room was at the rear, adjacent to the back door.

But it was Room 7 that I was interested in. It was hidden away down to the right off a badly lit corridor, all on its own. The water cooler was outside the door. To look purposeful, I pulled out the rubbish bag, which had ten or so empty paper cups inside, checked to see if anyone had noticed me, and turned the handle to Room 7 slowly. It was locked.

'You looking for something?'

Nurse Gabriella scared the shit out of me. 'Yes . . . no.' I held up the small bag of paper cups. 'I was just getting the rubbish.'

'You were trying to get in there.'

'Okay, I was curious.'

'It's not in use.'

'Why do they bring people to this room when they

die? Why not just leave them in their rooms till the undertaker comes?'

'What a morbid question.'

'Isn't that why Rose is scared of it?'

'Rose is scared of everything. And you, young lady, are wasting my time.'

Sticking out of her chest pocket was a black and gold fountain pen. So, maybe she was the anonymous weirdo in the logbooks. Creepy bitch.

'Go check on Nancy. She fell out of bed earlier today.'

As I made my way to Nancy's room, I wondered how this place was a viable business. Marcus obviously earned a fortune, but there were only seven rooms, four of them currently empty. Maybe he was doing it for the love of it. No! No one could love this job.

I'd spotted Nancy several times. In the activity room that first day, staring ahead, not even blinking (How weird is that, not even blinking), mouth slightly open, not moving a muscle. Then later that day in the garden, her husband wheeling her down the path, same face, no expression. And this morning, being fed a scone, her husband pushing her mouth open to pop a piece inside, then chewing in front of her in the hope that she'd copy him, and she did, but she still looked dead. Honestly, if her husband loved her, why didn't he crush twenty paracetamol into that scone? I would.

Maybe I should have knocked on Nancy and Gavin's

door. Promoting dignity should include knocking. I wish I had. Gavin had his shirt on, but no trousers or pants. His bony arse was bobbing up and down on top of Nancy's naked yellow flesh. Holy shit, the image of her face would never go away. It would stop me sleeping at night. Her eyes were wide open, not blinking. Her lips slanted downwards, slack. She wasn't moving a muscle. And her husband was having sex with her.

I shut the door and put my hand over my mouth in horror. What was that? Was it rape?

Nurse Gabriella was heading towards me. 'Is Nancy all right?'

'Yes. Well. Is Marcus around? I need to talk to him.' I didn't tell Nurse Gabriella. I realised by now there was no point talking to her about anything.

'He's writing upstairs and doesn't want to be interrupted.'

I waited till she was in the office then raced round the back, opened his door and yelled: 'Marcus! Marcus, are you there?'

'I'm in the office – come on up.'

When I blurted it out in a panic it didn't sound like something that required blurting or panic: 'I just walked in on Gavin having sex with his wife!'

Marcus was working at his PC on a huge polished walnut desk. This room was like the others – smooth and sterile, everything hidden.

He saved what he was doing. 'And?'

'And she's a vegetable! It's not right to have sex with a vegetable!'

He scratched his head. 'I see where you're coming from. I do, but they're married, and in her advanced care planning statement she said her sex life with Gavin was important to her.'

'In her what?'

'Advanced care planning statement. Like a death plan. And she said no matter what, that her sexuality was the thing she didn't want to lose.'

'But—' I didn't have my thoughts in order, but if I did, it probably would have sounded wrong anyway. She'd lost her sexuality, had she not? It had gone the way her blinking had gone.

'She was very clear about it. Look, I do understand where you're coming from. It's tricky. I'll check on Nancy. I'll talk to Gavin about it and I'll make a note of your concern.'

I felt nauseous but I wondered if I was just being stupid. The idea of any old married couple doing it made me slightly queasy, the queasiness increasing with the age of the couple in question. Maybe it was just my ageism that made it so horrific to me. Maybe all old people having sex looked like that. Blah . . . All I could say was: 'But . . .'

'I'll deal with it. Leave it with me. Are you okay?'

'Sure, just a bit shaken.'

'How 'bout a drink after work?'

*

The day went slowly after that. I watched Gavin wheel his wife around the garden, looking for signs of evil. He was gentle with her, loving. He sat on a garden bench and read to her. He moved a strand of hair that was in her eyes. He shooed a bee away from her arm. He walked her around and around, slowly. He seemed to care for her. But.

Nurse Gabriella noticed me staring out into the garden and sent me off to do several loads of washing. Ick. I wore gloves to put the clothes in the machine. Huge pants. Smelly socks. Wet trousers. After hanging them out, she suggested I listen to Jim play his guitar.

I didn't know any of the songs Jim sang but it wasn't agonising to listen to him, unlike two boys I dated who just happened to have their guitars at hand and ruined what might have been two perfectly good evenings. One sang obscure songs very quietly, maintaining intense eye contact, so I couldn't sing along and felt I had to listen. The other wrote a song for me called 'Feel It' – not dissimilar to Emma's rendition of 'The Bonnie Banks of Loch Lomond' in that it repeated one line over and over, and was very bad. (I didn't feel it again after that.)

Not Jim – he was good, a performer. I laughed, and joined in when required. I liked him. He was the most normal of the bunch, as far as I could tell. He asked me questions about myself and was interested in my answers. 'Costa Rica! Oh, wow! The grass there is to die for. Roll one for me, won't you, and dig into a huge platter of seafood after.' Plus, his life was fascinating. He'd toured with famous bands, although I'd never heard of any of them, and told stories about overdosing lead singers, about getting kicked out of hotels in Prague, about getting rich enough to retire one year, and blowing it all partying the next.

'So did you have groupies, Jim?'

'I had fun! Call me Jimmy. And listen, if you get any draw, will you bring me some?'

I found myself being professional. 'That's illegal. And bad for you.'

'Aw, c'mon, just enough for one joint. I'm on my way out anyway. I could do with a giggle.'

I promised I would, and made him promise not to tell.

He was funny, Jimmy – told me three jokes that all made sense and while I'd heard all three many years ago, it wasn't too difficult to conjure a laugh. I decided to spend as much time with Jimmy as possible. He was old right enough, but not in a stinky, crawls-on-the-ceiling kind of way. He didn't freak me out.

*

I had a lot of questions for Marcus and I didn't hold back when we got to the Brunswick Bar.

'Nurse Gabriella said you were writing?'

'Oh – aye, but don't tell anyone. Sounds kind of pathetic, a wannabe novelist. I tell you, I'm Googling some crazy stuff for the story I'm working on. And that, My Lord, is the case for the defence.'

We were drinking bright green cocktails in fancy glasses. I don't know what was in them, but they were strong and he was paying. 'So, where are your parents?'

'Retired to France two years ago. Left me the house and the business.'

'If you don't mind me asking, how does it make money, with so few patients?'

'The house is paid off, so that helps. And it's expensive, the fees. We get by.'

He was doing better than getting by. He drove a Mercedes FFS.

'But wouldn't you rather do something else?' Looking at him now, drinking cocktails in the bar like a normal young bloke, I could not imagine why he would choose to stay there. It wasn't as if he gave off caring vibes.

'That's why I'm writing! Hey, enough about me. Tell me the most embarrassing thing you've ever done.'

Maybe if I hadn't had two of those green drinks I

wouldn't have leant in as if to kiss him, then flicked his nostril: 'That.'

He flinched. 'Ow, I'm your boss, Miss Catherine.'

'And I'm your feisty wage slave, Mr Marcus.'

*

He dropped me off at six, saw me to my door, and kissed me like a gentleman, 'Goodnight, Catherine.'

Hmm. He was rich, he had a Merc, he was fun, he was my boss (which I found kinda naughty and naughty made me horny), but his kiss had inspired no tingles. That wasn't unusual, mind. The tingles had only happened once, with Paul, last summer. We were drunk, and alone at my place after a comedy night at The Stand. We were giving each other marks out of ten for certain parts of our bodies and were both being flirtatiously generous.

'Nine definitely!' He'd touched my legs.

I touched his chest. 'Nine.'

Lips were the last body part we marked. He said 'ten' as he moved in and I felt them: the tingles.

'Woah!' I jumped up from the sofa, scared to death by what had just happened. I felt something, for Paul. I couldn't afford to do that. He was the only real friend I had, the only one interesting and interested enough for me to be friends with for ever.

I told him to go, and he did. We never played that game again.

But I have two confessions. After the almost-kiss, I sat in bed and found myself writing him an email.

Paul,

I think I'll marry you, one day. You know that, don't you? So please do not attempt to kiss me again until I am thirty-nine.

C

The second confession is that I have written him an email every week since. That's thirty-six altogether. I never sent any of them, they're in the drafts folder. Some of them get quite soppy. Some of them get quite rude.

*

Mum was asleep when I got in. She'd obviously been tidying the house. It looked like there was hardly anything in it. No bits of paper on surfaces, no dirty clothes in the washing basket. She'd done one hell of a spring clean.

Ping, and Marcus had requested my friendship on Facebook. I deleted all the posts I'd done about work, and pressed Confirm. Yes, Marcus, we are now friends, and I am online and I am ready to chat.

Ping!

Ta for a fab night, Mx

Backatcha Cx

Sorry to talk work, but can you do 4 to 11 tomorrow instead of 9 to 4? And when you get in, don't go
in the front door, come upstairs first. I want to talk
to you before you start.

Right, so this wouldn't turn into a sex chat. I was glad –
I wasn't very good at those. Once you start them, there's
no going back so you have to pretend to be getting excited for at least twenty minutes (*Yes, I've taken my bra
off,* etc. etc.) and then pretend to come at the same time
as the person on the other end does and I'm not very
convincing. (*Yep, that's me too. Wow, amazing, seeya.*)
Okay, I messaged. *Everything all right?*

There was a long pause. Marcus was typing. Marcus
was still typing. Maybe he was on for a sex chat. I sighed,
got into bed, and prepared for twenty minutes of lying.
He was still typing . . . Shit, he wasn't going to get mushy
already, was he? Or feel the need to chuck me? I reassured him before his message came through.

No need to panic Marcus. I'm a laid-back chick.

After all that typing, this is all he wrote back. Must have deleted his first attempt, having seen mine.

> Not panicking! Remember to come upstairs first.
> Back door. See you at 4. ☺

*

Mum had gone to work by the time I woke. While I was making a pot of coffee, I noticed the menu on the fridge. She usually put up a weekly menu on Sundays, but today was Friday, and she'd done a new one for two full months. Eight weeks' worth, typed and printed and placed neatly under an Oxfam magnet beside the emergency numbers. She'd left a note on the table: *I love you Catherine. See you soon, my darling.*

She left notes like this every now again, when she felt guilty. I sat down to choose a cheerful movie that did not involve old people, icky sex or guilty mothers. *Blades of Glory* – perfect.

*

Five minutes into the film and I started thinking about Costa Rica. I could go any day now, which meant I'd have to tell Mum.

Plan A: Just leave her a note. *Bye Mum! Gone to see the*

world! I'll call when I can. After all, she left me notes all the time, didn't she? I grabbed the one she left for me and started composing a similar one: *I love you, Mum. See you soon.*

Plan B: Pack my bags and as I'm heading out to my preordered taxi tell her v casually that I'm off to find myself. Nah, she'd tell me she knew exactly where I was and that was 1. At home with 2. A huge credit-card bill and 3. No career prospects.

Therefore I should unpack those bags immediately and focus!

Plan C: Ask her to sit down with a glass of red and really talk to her. I could tell her I loved her, but that she controlled me, and that sometimes I felt a bit useless around her, like I was a disappointment and a mistake. I could say I needed some time alone; time to get to know myself, to be independent. Hmm. That might work. Maybe it was true, even.

I was a mistake, did I tell you that? My dad wasn't the one Mum married. He was the drug user she lived with beforehand. He died of an overdose in the one-bedroom flat they shared in Partick. 'He was a great person,' Mum would say. 'Creative and spontaneous and clever and funny!' They first met when he was studying English literature at uni while she was doing medicine. She flunked her final exams and spent the next few years with him as an unemployed hippy – i.e. smoking dope and marching against injusti: that's plural for any-old-issue. She was twenty-five and studying International Relations when he died. Mum had a small photo album which she'd mope over on his anniversary. One photo is of the two of them drinking in a campus bar. He had messy dark blonde hair and a huge toothy smile. My dad was a cutie pie – and I had inherited several pieces, with a big dollop of ice cream on top. God knows I didn't get my looks from Mum, ungracefully-grey non-smiler that she was. In another photo, they're in their living room. Their eyes were bloodshot – not, I suspect, the red-eye of the camera. A few friends were with them, strewn on the floor of what looked like a middle-class drug den (Victorian fireplace, polished floorboards, whisky bottles, bongs). Mum's drug problem was short lived, and limited to cannabis and the occasional trip. My father's got more serious. Impure street heroin had killed him. Apparently, Mum found him in the bath. He was smiling, Gran told me, with all those teeth of his. Way to go, Daddy-o. I don't blame his parents for not wanting anything to do with the bump in my mother's belly. The owner of that belly had led their son astray and then to death. She and her bump could fuck the hell off.

A year later, she married a man called Martin Watson, who built apartments on vacant Glasgow lots that had previously been used for burying bodies. He'd known her since she played Maria in *The Sound of Music* at the Eastfield Youth Theatre. He'd played the oldest son, Friedrich. He'd wanted to kiss her back then, but after four months of rehearsals and five 7.30 p.m. performances as her stepson, he started to feel wrong about it. Five years later, when she inspected one of his river-view penthouses, he finally had the courage to make a move. Gran was ecstatic, the marriage an excellent one. Soon, her daughter would don an apron and stand at the kitchen bench of a large Kelvindale townhouse, making Scottish Tablet with her first child while pregnant with her second. Alas, Mum got tired of Martin's traditional expectations and capitalist views after a year, and moved us out. I was two, so the only family unit I remember is me and my manic mum, who set about climbing the ranks of non-profit organisations, taking over, saving, the world.

*

'Your mother adores you, she's just torn between roles and role-modelling, like so many women are,' my gran told me when I was twelve. The hormones had kicked in and I'd run away to Gran's – seven blocks in total. We'd had an argument. Not the usual mother–daughter type like this:

Mother: You will not get a tattoo!

94

Daughter: Fuck you, I will if I want.

Mother: Don't swear.

Daughter: Why not? You do!

Mother: And I told you to tidy your room.

Daughter: Whatever.

No, no, Mum was too busy and too serious to waste time arguing about such things. These trivialities were agenda items, swiftly ticked during meetings at the dining room table. 'You won't get a tattoo? Good. 2: I'm not going to swear any more. You're right, it's a bad example. So you won't swear?' No pause before 'Good. 3: Sunday nights are a good time for you to tidy your room. This, Catherine, is something I would like you to do from now on.'

I got a tattoo when I was nineteen btw – Bacchus, the god of wine, in a black circle on the inside of my left biceps. Gina and Rebecca got Pegasus, but I thought that looked wank. I think they're jealous of mine now.

We didn't argue about tattoos, swearing, and tidying, but we did argue, like the time I ran away to Gran's. We yelled at each other about issues that Mum cared a great deal about, ones I didn't even know about, let alone give a toss. Refugees, the Middle East, female circumcision, for example. One night she had a dinner party with Antonio and a bunch of colleagues and made me join them.

I'd zoned out of the conversation, which was both dull and passionate. I was in the middle of a scintillating text chat with Gina about how chubby Rebecca was getting when Mum said: 'What do you think about the situation in Gaza, Catherine?'

'I don't think about it.'

'Shall I fill you in?' She'd gone bright red, angry. She'd probably guessed what I was going to say.

'Nah, you're all right.'

After everyone left, she yelled at me: 'You should be interested in the world! How can you be so self-absorbed?' She scratched a fresh list there and then: *1. Read at least two articles from the* Guardian *every morning. 2. Watch the* Channel 4 News *with me each evening. This. Catherine. Is something I would like you to do from now on!*

She threw the list at me, slammed the door.

But that wasn't the argument that made me run away to Gran's. That argument was about porn. She'd checked my browsing history and found the site I'd been viewing as a novice masturbator. Gina and Rebecca had been on at me to try it for a long time. You're so prudish, Catherine! God's sake, woman, get with the wank! They'd instructed me to use the shower head while thinking of Harry Groves in Third Year. No luck. Maybe because our shower head only reached as far as my belly and the spray wasn't forceful enough, or because the only image of Harry Groves that stuck was him eating a peach and it wasn't sexy at all, messy and kinda pukey – a lump of pink flesh stayed on his chin and I'm sure he noticed, but he didn't bother wiping it off. After several attempts to hone the shower head and the image of Harry Groves, they lent me a dildo and told me to use it in bed while thinking of Brendan Xavier from the telly. No luck (the dildo terrified me and Brendan Xavier's thick short eyebrows took up the whole screen in my fantasy. He looked like the devil.) After that they'd given me a bullet vibrator and the name of a porn site and instructed me to browse till I found something that worked. I'd tried a few times, but the sites had all made me a little queasy. Not sure I was into – or ready for – all that inside-out stuff. I don't know if I'd have kept on trying, but before I could even decide, Mum confronted me.

I was embarrassed, being caught, but livid at her response. She made me watch one of videos in front of her.

'Do you know who that girl is?' She'd paused the vid, pointed at the woman whose hair was being pulled, eyes open and looking up as a faceless man shoved himself down her throat.

'What?'

'Do you know how old she is?'

'How would I know?'

She zoomed in on her face. She had tanned skin, barely any make-up.

'Look at her. Eighteen? Seventeen? Maybe sixteen? Maybe younger. Look at her eyes. What do you see? Who do you think her mum is? You think her mum's seen this? Where do you think her home is, Catherine?'

I wanted to kill her. I'd need therapy about this later in life.

'She might have been kidnapped, trafficked, stolen. Her family might not know where she is. Or she might have been sold by her father. Or her neighbour might have paid her to do this, taken her to some strange house in some strange place and hit her if she didn't do what they told her to do. Do you know what her dreams are, Catherine? You know what's on her list?'

She'd zoomed in even closer but I was too angry to look. My mother's bullying righteousness was making me want to pay someone to kidnap and kill her. Also, I'd found Mum's bag of goodies in her bedroom cupboard – vibrator, videos.

'You are such a hypocrite, Mother! I've seen your porn stash.'

She blushed, paused. 'But I did my research. Those are made by women. This one here, what do you know about it? What do you know about her?'

'Why don't you watch the short interview with her

before the vid, Mother? Her name's Rixie and she's from Texas. She won best blowjob at the LA cock awards last year and wore a glittery gold gown! It's an industry, a business, and she "like totally loves her job!" Not everyone's dodgy, God!'

'Oh yeah? And in the interview did she say what's on her list?'

'Not everyone has fucking lists.'

'Maybe this week she wanted to train for a 5k run. Maybe she wanted to start learning to play the guitar. Maybe she wanted to try and stop swearing. Don't you realise that by watching this you're keeping that girl in that room? You're almost as bad as the traffickers who kidnapped her!'

'No one trafficked her! She's from Texas!'

I ran to Gran's. And I didn't get with the wank till I was seventeen. (And btw, it was always Paul I imagined. Worked every time.)

*

I loved spending time with Gran, I clung to her, relished her traditional maternalism. Her shortish dyed light-brown hair was always perfect. And right up till she died she wore foundation, mascara and lipstick, all the time. I think she even wore it to bed. She lost her husband when I was five. I don't remember him at all, but

Gran talked about him very affectionately. Apparently he made puns all the time, and believed eating out was a waste of time and money. ('He'd say: "My wife is a better damn cook than any restaurant chef!"') They had a happy marriage, Gran told me.

I often visited Gran after school. She would remove my stains and make me three-course meals from scratch, unlike Mum, who at that stage was always too busy during the week to make more than one-course meals from Marks and Spencer's.

I realise now that as much as I needed to spend time with Gran, I always went home afterwards, home to the mother who was not really a mother. And the reason I always went home, was that I wanted to. She and Gran were the two halves of me that hadn't quite fitted together yet.

I was eighteen when Gran died. Heart attack, it was. In the kitchen, apron on.

I believed my mother loved me in the same way as she'd loved Martin Watson. I was an attempt at conventionality that failed. I was even clingier than him, after all. I got in the way of several promotions. She told me so. 'I stayed in Glasgow for you, Catherine! London would have been a much better place, career-wise.' As it was, she had to commute there at least once a week after she'd reached director level. Gran was around the corner from ours, and I slept there when Mum was away,

moving myself back home on her return, often feeling a
nuisance and a mistake.

*

I'd go with Plan C: wine, chat, difficult truths. I decided
it would happen tonight after work, even checked we
had a bottle of her favourite Sangiovese in the cupboard.

On Skyscanner.net, flights to Costa Rica were around
£800. On the way to the travel agency, cash in pocket, I
ummed and ahhed about the best date to go. I know it's
callous, but one of the most significant factors was how
long Rose had left. I Googled dementia on my phone
in the taxi, but Marcus was right – there were many
different types of the illness, and I had no way of knowing how advanced hers was, although she was connected
quite often, so maybe not too advanced. If she lived another year, I could make a shedload more money and
have enough to travel the world for months. From what
I could gather, the old dear would probably not last
years, but may well hang around for at least another
twelve months. She was attached to me, and a lot of
the time thought I was Margie, so she might well keep
paying me to run pointless errands. I decided I should
stay at Dear Green for another month at least, and make
myself indispensable to her. I booked a one-way flight
to Costa Rica leaving in four weeks' time, making sure

it was a flexible ticket that I could change, in case the money was still rolling in and it was worth staying a while longer. I whistled all the way to Dear Green. Mistake-girl was getting outta here. She would be list-free, agenda-free, job-free, post-grad-in-social-work-free and mother-free.

*

An hour later I was by the river, screaming. I had run there shortly after saying 'Hey!' to Jimmy in Room 3. I had run as fast as I could, stopped when I reached the rocky bank, and screamed. I was never going to stop screaming. It felt too good to stop. I wish I'd done it aged five, when Mum made me make my own lunch before my first day at school; at twelve, when she made me go to the supermarket to buy tampons; at fifteen, when she dropped me at the sex clinic to so I could go on the pill, despite my assertions that I always used condoms and did not want to go in there alone and sit in a line with the prostitutes and drug users from Govanhill. I should have spent my life screaming at her. I was making up for it now.

I was so excited when I got to work – the ticket to Costa Rica in my wallet representing my new life – on planes, in jungles, on beaches, in cafés. I'd sorted out how to tell Mum and felt confident about it. I was so excited that I forgot Marcus had wanted to see me upstairs first.

I skipped in the front door, poked my head in to say hi to Rose, who was drawing at her table. She was in the present day, but looked worried, writing frantically. 'Are you okay, Rose?'

She put her pen down and her face transformed. I can't tell you how amazing these transformations were. Her face and body language became ten. Her eyes opened more widely, inquisitive, eager, optimistic. She held her back straighter. She fidgeted, jiggled a foot, bit at a fingernail. More than that, though. Her skin changed colour, from greyish-yellow to rosy pink.

She stood up easily, something she didn't do when she was old Rose, and ran over to me, grabbed my arms, kissed the top of my head. 'Margie, listen. I promise I'll be back. In an hour. I promise. I promise. I'll light a fire.'

She grabbed some drawing paper from the desk, ripped at it, scrunching pages into balls, then placed them on the floor at the foot of her bed. She put her pencils and brushes on top, teepee style. 'Matches! Wait, I'll run and get matches. Don't move.'

Holy shite, she was even crying like a kid, too. Not holding back, going for it. 'I won't let you die alone. I swear on Dad's life, I won't let you die! I'm just going to get matches.'

A couple of days ago, I'd have run off and hidden from this irksome display. I guess I'd changed a bit already. I smiled, and put my arms around her. 'I've got matches. I've got them. I know you won't leave me, Rose, I know. I know, it's all right.'

I put her in bed, touched her cheek. 'Everything's okay. I'm okay. I know you won't leave me. It's all okay.'

As I watched her relax and slowly close her eyes, I didn't see an old person who jumped the line to get on buses, paid for groceries slowly, took up space. I saw Rose Price.

She fell asleep.

Then I remembered. Marcus. Oops! I walked along the hall towards the back door, still happy, still excited. I waltzed past Room 4, and I'm sure I waved to Jimmy in the room opposite. He was strumming his guitar. I'm sure I said 'Hey there, Jimmy!' I'm sure as I was saying 'Hey there, Jimmy' I decided that I had just imagined seeing something in Room 4. A flash, a vision, from deep within my psyche, perhaps dug out because of the ticket I'd just bought, the escape I'd just planned. I don't know why I walked back to check if this was the case but I did so without any worry or concern, just a quick check. I walked back to Room 4. The door was half open. I opened it fully, expecting to shake my head with a 'silly me'. Alas, the image hadn't come from an imagination fuelled by guilt. My mother was in the room, sitting in the armchair by the window.

'Mum?'

'Catherine.' She'd said my name in an unusual way, as if 'Catherine' meant 'Help'.

'Did they say you could sit in here? What do you want?'

'Sit down, sit.'

'I'm working, Mum. You could have phoned me. Get up! I'll get in trouble.'

'Catherine, come and sit beside me.' She had a piece of paper in her hand and I could see the numbers on the left. She was wanting a meeting, with an agenda.

'Mother, I have no time for this now. I'm working. Whatever it is, let's talk about it when I get home. For God's sake, Gabriella's coming. She'll sack me.'

Gabriella had arrived at the door beside me. She gave my mother a kind smile, then touched my arm. 'You were supposed to go up and see Marcus before you started today.' Her voice was out-of-character gentle. I flicked her hand off my arm.

My mother bit her lip. 'I have to tell you something.'

'Well hurry, I have work to do. So do you. You should be at work.'

'Honey, nine weeks ago I was diagnosed with an aggressive brain tumour.'

I went like Nancy for a few minutes. Frozen. Maybe underneath Nancy's blank exterior, her brain raced like mine did in that moment. Three words from the sentence my mother had just spoken beat at my head. Diagnosed. Aggressive. Tumour. No, I thought. That doesn't make sense. My mother is a chairperson and a director and a righteous bossy boots who makes lists and saves lives and was okay last night, she was okay.

'Say that again.'

'Nine weeks ago I was diagnosed with an aggressive brain tumour.'

I repeated the sentence to myself. Brain tumours are deadly. Aggressive ones are deadlier. I noticed Mum's suitcase at the foot of the bed, a few of her clothes already on hangers in the open wardrobe, a photo of me on the bedside table.

'Baby, sit down. Come, sit beside me. I knew you'd want to look after me, but it's much better doing it here. This place has an excellent reputation. I looked into it thoroughly, and it's easy for you to get to. This is my home now.'

But I was supposed to move out of home first. But if this was her home, where was mine? But . . .

And then I ran to the river.

Three Weeks Prior to Death

CHAPTER EIGHT

AGE 82

Rose had been staring at her latest drawing for thirty minutes. Once again, she'd drawn Room 7. She'd drawn a camera in the corner. She was drifting, and she could tell, and she had to stop it. This had made sense to her, she was sure of it. Room 7. Camera. In the picture she'd just drawn, four figures were standing around the bed, obscuring the view of the person lying down. Only their backs were visible. She chanted in her head – *Stay Rose stay Rose stay Rose stay*. She read the caption beneath.

> *After intermission, the watchers returned to their game. Tilly was not pleased, but she was too exhausted now to complain.*
> *'Ah, Princess', said the Queen. 'So pretty, I fear I shall die a little death.'*

It was nonsense. It meant nothing. And if it was just a normal book, it was the worst she'd ever done. She berated herself. The thing she loved about being a writer was never having to retire. She knew writers who were still at it at ninety-five. She should be able to produce better work than this.

Unless this wasn't a book, unless she'd drawn these pictures for other reasons. Had she? Is that what this was?

Stay Rose stay Rose stay Rose stay.

She was not staying. She was going fast. She had to hurry. She put on the new Fly boots Chris had brought in for her and walked to the back of the house. No one noticed her going. They were all gathered in Room 4. Someone new had moved in, lucky thing, moving in to death. She opened the back door, went outside, and tried to open the window to Room 7. Painted shut, or locked, and the blinds were down. She gazed through a crack in the venetian. The room was bare. No camera. No people. Just a trolley bed, a bedside cabinet, a picture, wall rails, alarms, the usual. Perhaps if she got inside it she would find something that helped her understand her drawings.

*

AGE 10

Rose found a large stone, and tossed it through the window.

*

AGE 82

Things were swirly when she woke.

'How you feeling, Rose?' Marcus Baird, that's what the name tag said. Must be Marcus Baird standing over her now.

'What did you give me?'

'Just something to calm you down. You feeling calm?'

'I feel pissed is what I feel. Pissed off, that is.' She tried to sit up. 'What drug did you give me? Where's Natalie? Get Natalie!'

'Natalie left her job, remember? The doctor took a look at you and prescribed something to make you feel nice and happy.'

'Well it's not working.'

'Nice and happy, Rose.' Marcus Baird nodded to the nurse with the bright red lipstick. This place, these people, that's right!

The Queen, bright red lips.

Rose must have said or done something to make Marcus hold her down. She must have lashed out in some way perhaps, because he placed his hands on hers, while Nurse Gabriella prised her mouth open and put something in it. 'Drink it down, Rose, that's it, take a sip now, nice and calm.'

CHAPTER NINE

I was all out of screams by the time Marcus found me. He sat on the rocks beside me and stared where I was staring, at the field across the river. Several cows were in it. They looked relaxed. Stupid cows. They weren't for milking, they were for eating. That field was their hospice.

'So are you even paying my wage?'

He let out a short breath. 'No.'

I couldn't take my eyes off the cows. 'Isn't it against the rules, a relative of a patient working here?'

'No.'

'McDonald's has more rules than this place.'

'Your mum booked in nine weeks ago. She didn't want you to make the decision. Even big families find it an impossible thing to do, and you're on your own.'

'Why did she choose here?'

'Because it has an excellent reputation, and it's close to home.' Marcus had a file with him. 'Let me read you an email.' He opened the file and read from a piece of paper.

'Dear Mr Baird,

'Yesterday, Mr Hilary at Beatson Oncolocgy Centre diagnosed me with a brain tumour. As per notes attached, the type and position of the tumour make surgery impossible and treatment purely palliative. While radiotherapy may prolong the process for a few weeks, I have decided against it.

'I am a single mother. My daughter, Catherine, is twenty-three. She has no other family. I am writing for two reasons.

'One—'

I snorted. Even this email included a list.

'One,' Marcus continued. 'Dear Green comes highly recommended and if I am comfortable after having a thorough inspection of your resource, I would like to spend my final days there. If there is a place available, can you please email me immediately so I can visit as soon as possible? I would like to move in before my decreased mental capacities and mobility are obvious to Catherine.

'Two. I noticed online that you are looking for a care assistant. This may seem unusual, but my daughter is looking for a job and if you are happy with her CV and interview, I would like you to consider offering her a position. She doesn't realise this about herself, but she is very kind. She has always looked after me and I know she'll be an asset. I believe caring for me would be a much easier thing for her to do in a residential setting with the support of trained staff. I would, of course, cover the costs of her employment.'

'You should have told me.'

Marcus bit his lip. 'Should I? I was torn, believe me. But I could understand where she was coming from. You wouldn't believe how hard it is for families to make the hospice decision. You would have battled along to the point of collapse. You'd have wasted the time you have with her. You'd have been no good to anyone. This way is easier; I agree with her. Your mother's amazing, Catherine.'

The desire to cry gave way to anger again. 'She's a control freak.'

'Here, read through her file. Maybe it'll help.'

Marcus put his hand on mine. 'I have to get back. Rose just tossed a rock through a window.'

'A rock?'

'Yeah, Room 7.'

'Is she okay?'

'She's sedated, sleeping now.'

He smiled sadly and left.

*

I don't know how long I'd been walking before I found the tree on the river-bend that Rose always ran away to. I sat with my back against it, like wee Margie, and the tears came. Eventually, I opened the file Marcus gave me. There were emails. Yes, she could visit. Yes, she was impressed. Yes, there was a place. Yes, she wanted it. Yes, she had filled in all the forms, paid all the money. Yes, the interview went well, the job mine. Yes, they wouldn't tell me, or press me too hard. Yes, yes, yes.

There was a document titled 'Advanced Care Planning'. It was signed at the bottom by someone called Adrienne Malloy and also by my mother. She had given medical and financial power of attorney to me. For most of the other questions on the form, Adrienne Malloy had written: 'See patient statement attached.'

This is what my mother wrote:

1. I don't want counselling, I know how I feel and exactly what I want.

2. I don't want to be resuscitated if I stop breathing from this moment on.

3. I don't want to be force fed or hydrated. If I stop eating and drinking, so be it.

4. I want to die at Dear Green Care Home, not at home.

5. I do not want to go home at all once I have moved in. My home should remain a happy place, with happy memories.

6. I don't want my daughter to be with me when I'm

in the final forty-eight hours because it can be noisy and ugly and she does not need to hear or see that.

7. I don't want or need to go to hospital. Whatever happens, happens in my room in Dear Green.

8. I don't care about having music or any particular people or anything sentimental around me when I am nearing death. I'll most likely be in a coma, it won't matter to me.

9. I'm not religious and I don't want the last rites, but if my daughter suddenly feels strongly about it then I don't mind.

10. I'd like as much pain relief as I need to be as comfortable as possible.

11. I do not want my daughter to see my dead body. I saw my mother's and it's the image of her that I remember most to this day. I wish I could un-see it. My daughter may want to see it. Say no.

12. In terms of the funeral, I don't care whether I'm cremated, buried or tossed in the sea. I have bought an eco-friendly coffin and organised what I think would be suitable and manageable, but if my daughter would like to change anything, she can. I want her to do what she feels is right for her.

There were several envelopes – Mortgage (recently paid off). House (now in my name). Car (paid off, in my name). Savings (£32k, transferred to a new account in my name). Household Bills (direct debits set up to my new account). Will and lawyer's details (everything to me). Coffin (paid for, to be collected from a man called Eddie, who'd been very helpful indeed). Funeral Director (contact details). And there was the name and address of my father's parents (in case Catherine ever decides she wants to meet them).

I remember asking Mum about my birth once. Think I was around nineteen. Truth be told, contraceptive failures had occurred and I thought I was pregnant at the time and while I'd decided not to keep it if I was, my head was buzzing with millions of questions.

I should have known she wouldn't be one of those women who lie about it. It was lovely! It was over in a day! As soon as you came out, I forgot the pain! Instead: 'It was the most excruciating experience of my life. Like someone stabbing you in the stomach with a very sharp knife and twisting it for a minute, then doing it again two minutes later. For twenty-six hours. Can you imagine? I had a birth plan. I'd been to all the classes on offer and decided I wanted a water birth and no pain relief. So I sat in the bath for twenty-six hours, screaming. I think I was waiting for them to take control and inject me with something, I'd lost the thinking power to ask for drugs, and they never offered. Turned out it was because of that bloody birth plan.'

I can just imagine how detailed it was. A list of exactly

how she wanted it to go, just like this. But then, like now, she hadn't factored in that time can change you, circumstances can change you, pain and fear can change you.

Whenever I think of myself in a past event – I dunno, snogging some guy at a bar, cramming for Higher Maths at the last minute, breaking my arm falling off the climbing frame in Maxwell Park – I see someone else entirely. That person wasn't me. I don't even recognise her. This idea has comforted me through the years, because I know that whatever's in store for me (like childbirth, for example) will be dealt with by another-me altogether. So how can present-me know what's best for future-me?

Mum hadn't factored me into her birth plan. I did not want to come out. It took an emergency Caesarean section in the end, so she wound up having twenty-six hours of excruciating pain in a revolting plastic tepid bath, followed by the highest level of pain relief and medical intervention that is possible.

You think she'd have learned by now that some things are not within your control. Some things can't be planned. That the person she is now is not necessarily the person she will be tomorrow.

After talking to Mum about childbirth I decided to keep the baby if I was pregnant.

I started my period the following morning.

I s'pose a daughter shouldn't run away from her mother at a time like this, shouldn't scream with rage by a river, shouldn't want to go as far away as possible and never face her again. But most daughters wouldn't be lied to. She should have let me see her symptoms, not hidden them behind fake menopause, fake pins and needles. She should have taken me along with her to the doctor. I would have argued with him or her, insisted on second and third opinions, Googled and phoned and emailed and written and fought. I would have forced the radio-therapy on her, researched homeopathic solutions and foods and I dunno what else, but I'd have tried. And she didn't trust me, didn't even let me. Now it was too late and she was going to die and that was going to ruin my life. My life. That was what I was thinking about. Mine, not hers. I was shaking. I was thinking of ways to make this go away. I could run. I was a fast runner in emergencies – when getting the last bus back from town, for example. Perhaps if I ran, this would pour out of my armpits and pound into the ground. That's what I'd do, run. I took off across the field and lasted about a minute. No sweat, no pounding, just the realisation that fear was driving me away more than anger, and that I should stop. I lay on the grass. Two cows were within feet of me, and I wasn't scared of them, just her, of seeing her and talking to her. She was no longer the person I'd always known. The person who was in control, annoying, bossy, not dying. Now, she was someone entirely different.

But I couldn't face her yet. I didn't want to go inside that death building. I didn't want to go home. I needed to talk to someone. Rebecca was online on Facebook chat, so I sat up on my muddy mound and messaged:

You around? Need to talk.

Doing a facial. In 15?

My friendships and my crises had all been played out and managed on Facebook. I didn't think for a moment before typing:

My fucking mum's dying. Brain tumour.

The reply:

Geez, so sorry ☹

Perhaps Facebook was the wrong forum for this. I dialled Gina's mobile. 'Can you talk?'

'Aye. Just – Will, turn that off! TURN IT OFF! Sorry, can't hear. Turn it off, you wanker!'

In the background: 'Just go to the other room!'

'Why should I?'

A scuffle, a door shutting. 'That arsehole. You know he fraped me last night – said I love . . .'

'Gina, I just found out my mum's got a brain tumour.'

Silence for a moment. 'Oh my God, no.'

'I know, I can't believe it.'

'God, I'm in shock . . .' A long pause. Gina was not good at this. I didn't fill it. 'Will she lose her hair?'

I hung up, dialled a taxi, walked to the main road, and went to Paul's house.

Of course he wasn't in. 'He's at the library till five today,' his grandfather said. 'You want to play cards till he's back?'

Halfway back to Dear Green, I changed my mind and asked the driver to take me to Gartmore.

*

'Mum's dying.' I blurted it out to an almost complete stranger, just like that. Unlike a stranger, Chris hugged me, helped me inside.

'She moved in next to Rose today and I didn't even know she was sick. That's why she made me get the job. She should have told me.' I couldn't get any more words out, just tears. Inside, all I could think was: *She's going to die. My mum's going to die.*

A few tissues later, I calmed down a bit. 'I'm sorry. I shouldn't have come here like this. I don't know you at all.'

He filled the kettle. 'Don't be daft. People who haven't been through it don't understand, they say all the wrong things. My best friend in the world, you know what he said when Gran went in? When I'd phoned him, crying?'

I shook my head.

'"Well, she's had a good life." I wanted to kill him. I've had a good life, but I don't want to be in a hospice with advanced dementia, reliving a real-life nightmare over and over, only waking from it to find yourself in another one!'

'My friends are all idiots.'

He smiled. We were friends. 'So, you found out, then ran off?'

'Yeah.'

'You need to go and talk to her.'

I nodded. I would. But not while I was feeling angry. I had to calm down.

'You don't need to keep working there if you don't want to.'

That hadn't even crossed my mind. 'Don't know how I feel about anything. I've spent my life trying to rebel against her organisation of me, and it's like that's all I know how to do. I can't believe she hid it from me.

What kind of person hides that from her child, her only family!'

But I shouldn't have been surprised. Mum always planned and controlled things, and the basis for every decision she made was my happiness. She did this for me.

Chris sat on the sofa, patted the seat beside him for me to sit.

'Margie's death changed my gran's life. She could never let it go. I think it defined her as a person. She'd let her down. She'd left her alone. She'd broken a promise. She'd failed.'

I knew what he was trying to tell me: square things up now, before it's too late. Don't have any unfinished business. Say a loving goodbye, make it perfect, make it one you can live with. Do what Rose hadn't managed to do with Margie.

'It's important to get this right. This time with your mum will stay with you for ever.'

When I look back over everything that happened at Dear Green, almost every day seemed like a major turning point for me. But the moment I'm most thankful for is when I realised Chris was right. There was no time for me to mature, no time to work through my resentment and my selfishness, no time for Mum and me to journey towards an understanding and acceptance of each other and of the past. If I didn't get on with it now, make the most of her, put my anger at how she'd approached this behind me, then I'd regret it for the rest of my life. I grew up in Chris's living room that day. I only had my mum. I loved her. And she only had me. She was going to die, and soon. She wouldn't get the chance to annoy me by boycotting my wedding or by forcing me to compromise by organising a humanist, feminist one. I wouldn't get to see her turn all earth-mothery as a grandmother, donning an apron, sewing buttons, baking scones, doing stuff she never did with me. No, our story had come to an end.

Chris's phone rang and I knew immediately that something was wrong. He hung up and grabbed his car keys. 'I've got to go. Gran ran away again.'

'Where is she?'

'Maryhill Police Station. I'll drop you off.'

I wasn't in awe of Chris any more. He made me feel safe and calm. Lucky Rose, having a grandson like him. As we drove towards Glasgow, I wondered if I could be as good at caring as he was. What would be required of me? What would Mum expect? Would she cry all the time, get angry at me, angry at the tumour, angry at death? I felt sick with terror. I was about to enter a terrible time. It could last days, weeks, months. Worse than terrible. And after that ... what, after that? I tried a technique Mum had taught me in the early secondary years, when low moods had started arriving at least once a month. 'If something's worrying or upsetting you, just don't think about it. Say this to yourself: "I'm not going to think about that."'

I tried this, in the car. It didn't work. It was impossible and wrong not to think about this.

'You okay there?' Chris had heard my teeth grinding.

'Not really.'

'Want to talk about it?'

'I don't think I do.'

*

I stayed in the car while Chris collected his gran. Yesterday, everything around me had seemed simple and pretty: who to have drinks with, where to go on holiday, who to kiss, who liked my Facebook posts. Today: lies, illness, death. And there was Rose, her arm through Chris's as he escorted her back to the car. She was so tiny – smaller than me even. She looked confused and angry.

'In you go, that's it, Gran.' Chris buckled her in the back seat. As we drove to Dear Green, he filled me in on what had happened.

She'd hailed a taxi on the main road in front of the garage. The driver said she was very anxious, desperate to get to the station with some information that would save lives. Actually, what she said exactly was that she had information that would 'save deaths', but the taxi driver figured she was confused. And he was right. By the time he had delivered her to the police station, she couldn't recall why she was there. She had the drawing in her hand. She'd looked at it and said: 'This isn't publishable!' She shook her head in dismay, apparently. 'I've lost it. I can't write or draw any more. I'm a useless idiot.'

Chris knew two of the police officers. He'd been in the station speaking to them for a long time, which suited me because I didn't feel ready to face Mum yet. I was practising what to say, how to act. I was imagining how to make her feel calm, while hiding my own panic. I was forming a list in my head, making a plan. After hugging her, holding her, telling her I loved her, I'd head home and get her favourite music, the laptop, some DVDs she'd always been too busy to watch. I'd get some strawberries – she adored strawberries. And cream. She could eat all the cream she wanted, damn it. I'd buy some nice oils and give her massages. I'd get the *Guardian* and read it to her! I'd get the *Guardian* every day, read it to her every day! Oh, and we'd watch the *Channel 4 News* together and I'd concentrate on what they were saying and we'd discuss the items afterwards. And we'd go for walks around the garden. I'd hold her hand.

*

Rose was very fidgety in the back seat, and took one of

her shoes off en route to Dear Green. 'This is the ugliest anklet I've ever seen. Who gave me this?'

She had a contraption around her ankle. It was obviously irritating her. She was trying to pull it off, and failing. 'Get this off!'

'Gran, I explained in there. If you wear that, I'll always know where you are.'

'But I don't want you to always know where I am.'

'Is that an electronic tag?' Surely not, I thought.

'It's hush-hush, okay. I pulled in some favours. I know it's difficult to get your head around. But how do I keep her safe? It makes sense. I can track her on my phone.'

She was yanking at it. 'It won't come off!'

'No, Gran, it stays on.'

She was still yanking at it by the time we arrived.

I felt numb approaching the house. My mum was in there. And she was dying. As Chris took Rose inside, I stopped at the front door and began sobbing uncontrollably. I sat on the step and composed myself. She shouldn't see me cry.

I needed to be strong.

CHAPTER TEN

AGE 82

Sometimes Rose didn't like Chris. He was very bossy with her. Do this do that, put this on, take that off, sign this, don't go out, sign that, wear this. Sometimes she wished he would go away. Like now. Bossy little boy. She wanted to take the ankle bracelet off and he wouldn't let her. She'd have to wait till he left and cut it with scissors. His mother should have set some boundaries when he was younger. She should not have given him everything he wanted. 'Where's your mother?'

'She lives in London, you remember?'

She did remember. Of course she did. What did he think – that she'd lost her mind?

'You can't keep running away, Gran. They can't keep fetching you.'

Ooh, this kind of talk really peeved her. She was a grown-up woman, very grown-up. She would bloody well run away if she wanted to. She didn't have children to care for any more. She earned her own living. She could run away any time she wanted, and it wouldn't be running away, it would just be going somewhere. She could go somewhere now, if she chose to, even if she didn't know why or where to.

Rose was glad when she saw the dull girl walk past her room. 'Hey! You! Come here. Tell my grandson to go home.'

The girl seemed sad. She walked in, reluctantly. 'Go home, Chris! You heard the woman.'

'Right, I will then, Gran. I'll be back tomorrow.' He kissed her on the forehead, then kissed the dull girl on the cheek, and left.

Sometimes Rose really couldn't stand him, you know. He reminded her of a guinea pig. Scratchy and jittery, always wanting human food: gimme, gimme.

Rose opened her bedside cabinet and retrieved a toilet bag. 'They've taken my nail scissors! Jesus Christ, what's going on here? They can't just take my things. Have you got some scissors?' Rose tugged at the contraption on her ankle. 'I cannot work out the latch on this ugly thing.' The girl was crying. 'You're not allowed to cry. You work here.'

The girl flicked through her drawings, nervous, worried. 'What was your latest drawing? You were taking it to the police.'

'Oh I don't know. Stupid. I'm ashamed of it.' Rose picked it up and read with a mocking tone:

'"After intermission, blah, blah, blah." What is that? My career is over.'

The girl looked at the page and smiled. 'Nah, you just need to keep working on it.'

'True indeed! Writing is rewriting. Maybe you're not so dumb after all.'

'You thought I was dumb?'

'More dull than dumb, actually. I thought there was nothing to you.' The girl was very on edge. Maybe Rose shouldn't have said that. She always said things she shouldn't. People didn't need to know every little thought in her head. But being a famous writer had required spontaneous over-sharing. The books were the thoughts in her head, after all. And the newspaper, magazine and radio interviewers all asked her about the little thoughts in her head. For years, all she did was talk about herself, and the thoughts in her head. 'Sorry, I didn't mean to upset you.'

'No, you're right.' She crossed her arms and scratched at her shoulder. 'My mum's moved in next door. I just found out she has a brain tumour.'

Like it or not, then, the girl would be forced into depth. Rose felt compelled to hug her. Right now, she reminded her of Margie, so like Margie. Was it her eyes?

'I need to go talk to her. I kind of ran off.'

But she wasn't going. She was sobbing again. Rose took her in her arms and held her until she calmed. 'Sit here for a few minutes before you go in. Sit down and tell me about your mum. What's she like?'

'She hates men and motherhood, a feminist. I was a mistake.'

'I love men and motherhood and I'm a feminist.'

'Well she doesn't love or need either. She brought me up to be the same.'

'I can understand. I did the same for my girls to a certain extent. It was hard to get a balance. One of my daughters, Elena, doesn't need them at all – she's a lesbian, doesn't hate them, mind; just doesn't need cock.'

The girl stared.

'What was I saying? My other daughter, Chris's mum, hates her husband so much she often wants to murder him and I wouldn't object if she did. She and her husband move invisible money around for a living. Makes no sense to me, but it means they're able to buy loads of stuff. All the stuff in the world, yet they never have anything interesting to say.'

The girl laughed. She had a lovely laugh. 'I'd better go. Mum's next door, like I said.'

'Okay. Hey, don't let this take over.'

'What?'

'That she's dying. Remember that she's living.'

'Thanks, Rose. I'll pop in on you later.'

'Oh, and, girl!'

'Yeah?'

'Can you get me some scissors?'

CHAPTER ELEVEN

I stood outside Mum's door for a few minutes because I couldn't stop crying. My mother was dying. I said it over and over in my head. *My mother is dying my mother is dying.* When I was little I used to fantasise that I got very bad news in a public place, and my friends would feel sorry for me and I'd be kind of famous. In my fantasies, the head teacher would call me out of class, or I'd get a phone call while on the school bus. Everyone would stare at me. I liked the idea. It comforted me, sent me to sleep. *My mum is dying my mum is dying my mum is dying.* No fame, and no comfort, in this nonsensical sentence. I decided to try my mum's advice again ('Just don't think about it'), as thinking about it was making me cry even harder. I took three deep breaths, knocked on the door, and went inside.

She was sleeping, or at least she had her eyes shut. I stood at the side of the bed and looked over her. How could I have not noticed? She'd been dragging her left foot around the house for weeks. She'd not been at work (working from home my arse). She'd fallen over at least once that I knew of. ('Silly me!' she'd say.) She'd packed the house and made enough food for me for a year. She'd been crying a lot. And there was that 'episode' about a month ago. I'd arrived home from the pub to find her unable to move on the bathroom floor. She told me she'd had too much to drink, and I'd believed her. (How stupid was I? Mum never got drunk to the point of paralysed.) It took me about an hour to get her into the bed. And now, even though she was sleeping, I could see that she had changed dramatically. She was drenched in sweat. Her face was puffy – she'd gained weight.

She opened her eyes. 'Hello.'

'Hey, Mum.' I took her hand and kissed it.

She stared at me. 'Catherine.'

'Yeah.'

'You're mad at me.'

'I was, not now. I'm here for you, just like you wanted. I've read your plan and I want you to know I'm okay with all of it. I'll make sure things go exactly the way you want.'

Her lip quivered. 'This isn't the way I wanted things to go at all.'

The quiver didn't turn into a cry. She was holding it in. I put my head on her chest. 'Me either.'

I'd always preferred Mum when she was sick. She stayed still. Once, feverish with a chest infection, she even watched a whole movie without budging. I kept my head on her chest, and could feel as she relaxed into sleep. I did the same, later waking to her voice.

'Where did all this furniture come from?'

'Hi there. What furniture?'

She tried to sit up, but couldn't. I grabbed her arms and hauled her upright. It took all my strength. How could she have deteriorated so fast? Had she given in to it by moving here?

'It's weird, being here again.'

'Have you been in this room before?'

As well as the puffy face, her eyes were glassy and her mouth didn't seem capable of smiling or frowning. She stared in a blank, confused way. 'I need to go to the toilet.'

And thus began a routine so consumed by the frantic needs of a failing body and mind that there was no time, and no need, for crying.

*

When I introduced Mum and Rose the day after Mum moved in, I assumed they'd get along, even form some kind of self-help alliance for strong independent women with rotting brains. And they did, the first time they met.

'No one listens to me any more,' Rose's hand was shaking. 'They took my only friend away, you know. Her name's Natalie and she has the most beautiful family, four boys. She tries to come and they stop her. Are you listening?'

Mum had made a career out of listening to the disenfranchised. 'Yes, of course I am.'

When Rose left the room, Mum made me promise that I wouldn't dismiss everything Rose said. 'Listen to people without voices, won't you, Catherine, from now on?'

I promised.

The following day, Rose popped in again while I was giving Mum her lunch. She'd shut the door and asked if she could use Mum's phone. 'Natalie? It's Rose, you have to help me. Oh, damn answering machine!' She hung up and called the police. 'This is Rose Price,' she'd said. 'I am phoning from Dear Green Care Home in Clydebank. Please take note of what I'm saying. People are dying here, and not the way you think. What I mean is . . . I'm trying to explain! If you'd just let me explain . . . There's evil here! I've asked and asked for you to investigate this place. Have you looked into the people here? I told you, my name is Rose Price. Yes, I know I've been in touch before. You stupid cunt, I'm telling you to do something!'

I wasn't sure what to do, so I pressed Mum's buzzer. Nurse Gabriella came in, snatched the phone from a now-hysterical Rose, assured the police that no one was in danger at all, that Rose was confused and that, yes, they would make sure she didn't waste police time again.

'Poor thing,' Mum said when Nurse Gabriella and Marcus had carried her – kicking and screaming – back to her room.

Marcus came back in a while later. 'We've locked Rose's door from the outside. No other way, I'm afraid, but we do hear her if she needs us. You won't be having any unexpected visits from now on.'

'Can you check on her every hour?' Mum asked me after he'd left. 'So sad.'

*

The week before Mum moved in, the doctor had upped her dosage of steroids. That's why her mobility had gone downhill so rapidly, and why her appetite and weight had increased. It also caused the sweating. I found myself changing Mum's T-shirt every hour, and helping her walk as far as seemed manageable, which wasn't very far. (Enter Zimmer frame and step-by-step instructions: That's it, that's it, one hand on one handle, one on the other, now push yourself up! Yay, well done! Now right foot first, just one step, back straight, look ahead, good!)

It was the toilet thing that I found the hardest. I'd seen her pee, but never the other. And it took a while to get my head around it. At first, I'd stand at the bathroom door and peek at parts that were dressed, telling myself I could dash in if she looked like falling. But soon I discovered that I couldn't dash in fast enough. She fell moving from loo to sink, trousers still at her ankles. Getting her up again was much more difficult than I imagined. We were knotted there on the floor together for ages before I thought through how to go about it (try and get into a kneeling position, hand on toilet seat, and up). After that, I had to go in there with her, pulling her pants down, getting her into position and watching while she did the business and while she wiped.

I never knew my mum used so much toilet paper, and that she folded it, very neatly. I was happier not knowing.

*

It had been five days since Mum moved in, and I hadn't left Dear Green at all. Mum was asleep. Nurse Gabriella had gone home, and Harriet was in the television room. If this was where my mum was to spend her last days, I wanted to know everything I could about it, and this was the first chance I'd had to take a closer look. I closed the office door and checked through the filing cabinets, curious about the people here, especially Nurse Gabriella and her fountain pen.

Her file included a copy of her nursing qualification, her Disclosure Scotland certificate, her bank details, and her CV. She was fifty-six, divorced and had no criminal convictions. On the personal statement in her CV, she'd written that her son's death had changed her life and inspired her to work with the dying. Someone had written in red pen beside this statement – 'Article in *Herald*, Dignitas.'

I googled 'Gabriella Nelson' and 'Dignitas' and 'Herald' and clicked on the article.

Mother's failed attempt at euthanasia

After caring for her terminally ill son for eighteen months, Gabriella Nelson was denied medical approval to take her only child to the Dignitas clinic in Switzerland. 'I tried because he begged me to,' Gabriella Nelson explained. 'He couldn't stand the pain.' David Nelson, twenty-three, was diagnosed with lymph node cancer of the head and neck. After one operation and two failed bouts of chemotherapy, personal trainer and rugby player David was given three months to live by doctors at the Beatson Oncology Unit. David was admitted to the Southern General Hospital three days ago, and died there at 5.30 a.m. yesterday. 'It was not what he wanted,' Ms Nelson says. 'It was not peaceful.'

The grief-stricken mother in this article didn't feel like the curt woman with the nurse's badge. So very sad. But also strange and creepy that she came to work here afterwards.

The other staff and resident files were less intriguing.

Tubby, ugly care assistant Harriet had never married, and spent her life cleaning people's houses before starting here ten years ago.

The part-time care assistant, Molly, was twenty-eight, and in a long-term relationship with the father of her two children, both under ten.

Catatonic Nancy and her husband Gavin had been married forty-one years. They had three children and seven grandchildren. She'd been a receptionist, he an accountant. Her advanced care planning statement was in her file, and read just like Marcus said. 'Sex is very important to me and Gavin. No one and nothing can take that away from us.'

I was about to read Jimmy's file (his surname was Thornton) when I heard banging. It was Rose, trying to get out of her room again. 'Help me! I'm being held prisoner!' she was yelling. The noise had woken Harriet, who gave her a tranquilliser and settled her back into bed. It had also woken Mum, who had tried to get up to help Rose, and was now lying face down on the floor.

Every hour since she arrived, Mum's situation

changed, and I had very little time to think about anything else. I'd find a routine that worked for whatever basic function we were trying to achieve, and then bang, something went wrong and I had to work out a whole new one.

In five days, she went from being able to walk to the dining room to not being able; from being able to wipe her own bottom to not being able; from being able to get out of the bed on her own to falling on the floor with a thud; from being able to get up off the floor to not. So I'd update my system, chuck out the piece of equipment we'd been using, and find another one to suit the short-lived stage we now found ourselves in. I kept busy, working out equipment, making her comfortable, talking happy talk, avoiding conversations that might remind her of where she was and why she was there.

Other activities punctuated the days. A harpist came and played one evening. A tear machine, that instrument. The guy, Pete, spent his weekends playing his music for the dying. I left the room, walked to my regular spot on the river, and sobbed.

There were visits from massage therapists, physiotherapists, oncologists, occupational therapists and aromatherapists. I escaped upstairs to Marcus's for a nap when someone else was with Mum, but I never managed more than a couple of hours at a time. I needed sleep but I didn't want it. As soon as I lost sight of her, I panicked, felt lost and terrified. Being with her and helping her was the only way to keep my head.

Aggressive was the right word for this tumour. Sometimes I'd look at her head, imagining the killer within it, wishing I could suck it out through her ears, massage it out with my hands, will it out with my tumour-free mind. Other times I'd look at her head and refuse to believe there was anything unusual going on inside it.

I was helping Mum back into bed when the doctor arrived. Mum had decided she was tired of the sweating and the immobility and the mouth ulcers caused by the steroids. 'I'd prefer the swelling to this,' she told the doctor, who was around forty, I'd say; a cougar. 'No more medication, just pain relief if and when.'

'So no more steroids?' The doctor's expression said it all. (*Do you know what this will do? Are you sure?*)

Mum's face answered the questions. The answer to both was yes. She nodded. 'No more steroids.'

I wonder why I didn't realise the significance of it. The loss of mobility had seemed so awful, I couldn't imagine anything would be worse. I suppose she believed the same. I wish I'd known that morning, that this was the last day I would be able to talk to her, really talk. I should have let her cry, let her see me cry. I should not have prioritised my fears above hers, and stifled the only opportunity I'd ever have to tell her how much I admired and loved her. I should have let her be afraid. I should have lay beside her and wept with her for hours and hours before the swelling came and took her from me. I should have made her stay on the steroids.

After the doctor left, a girl called Zoe came to massage Mum's feet (although Mum couldn't feel it. Her feet had died already. Death was taking over from the bottom up.) I went upstairs to make an attempt at sleep and Marcus offered me a joint. Ah, just what the care assistant ordered. Perhaps drugs would quell the terror and the sadness. I smoked half of it, head out of the drawing-room window, and slept for three hours.

Since Mum's arrival, I'd avoided everyone except Rose. As I walked back to Mum's room, I popped in on Jimmy.

'I have a present for you.' He was sitting in bed, guitar in hand. I passed him the unsmoked half of the joint.

'Oh my! I knew I loved you from the moment I saw you. Now, it's an obsessive love!'

'Have it outside, yeah? You want me to take you?'

'No, I'm fine. I'll nip out myself when everyone's busy with the new boy.'

'New boy?'

'Not new exactly. He was here a month, then went home for a few days. He's going fast; family had hoped he'd go at home, but they couldn't cope. That's him arriving.'

I guessed it was his parents wheeling him down the hall. They looked exhausted and devastated, but were trying to maintain some normalcy by chatting about practicalities. 'We'll set up the laptop on the lunch tray,' his mother said. 'You can keep Skype on all the time,' his father said. 'I'll point our camera at the kitchen so you can see what we're up to.' The boy, just twenty-one, wore a black Billabong beanie, his thin legs covered with a blanket.

'That's a great idea.' His voice wasn't a flat, dying voice. He really did think that was a great idea.

It struck me that the dying cared for the carers almost as much as the other way round. Mum was always telling me to rest, saying thanks, keeping her voice as animated as possible, being grateful, never talking about the truth of what was going on, the horror of her loss of self and of what was to come. She was always agreeing that whatever small alteration I had made in the room, or to her clothing, was excellent, perfect, just right. Aren't you clever! That's a great idea!

Jimmy sighed as the boy's bedroom door was shut. 'Leukaemia, wee soul.'

I was becoming uncomfortably comfortable talking about illness. 'What's wrong with you, Jimmy?'

He sniggered. 'What's wrong with me is that I'm old

143

and no one wants me. I could be here for years.'

'In that case –' I pointed to the joint in his hand '– I'd better get you some more of those!'

*

Mum was asleep again. I knocked on Rose's door and unlocked it. As usual for this time of the day, she was at her desk, drawing.

'Catherine! I'm just finishing off a drawing. I want you to do a job for me.'

I looked at the page. Again, Room 7. But this time the room was crammed full of faceless people, swirled together in an angry mess. Once again, one of the blank faces had bright lipstick, but she'd drawn no other facial features. A small bony figure lay on the bed.

I read the words out loud.

Tilly wasn't just sick of the game of Kings and Queens, she was actually sick. And so young. A crowd would gather by her bed when the time came.

'Here's five hundred. Take it to Natalie Holland. That's her home address. She's cluey. She'll understand. Tell her—'

'—the truth is in your drawings.'

'Yes! How did you know that?'

'You've asked me to go to her before, Rose.'

She put her head in her hands, annoyed, then shook it

off, folded the page. 'Maybe she'll understand this one. Tell her—'

'—the truth is in your drawings, I'll tell her.'

'You have to go now, because of Jason. Hurry!'

I assumed Jason was the young guy I'd just seen moving back into Room 5.

'I can't take your money again, Rose.'

'No, you can't.' The voice was Chris's. He was standing at the door behind me, and had obviously heard our conversation.

'Just how much have you taken from my grandmother already?'

'Um. Oh shit.' It was awful what I'd done, wasn't it? I decided to be completely honest. 'One thousand five hundred. I'll give it back. I'm sorry.'

He nodded, his lips tight and angry. 'You will, yes. And I'm going to report you, Catherine. I'm gobsmacked. I am absolutely appalled. Where are you hiding money, Gran?'

'It's none of your business. It's mine.' Rose was a tough old bird when she needed to be.

'I know, but it should be in the bank. I'm keeping it safe for you. Do you have a hiding place? Where are you hiding things?'

'What things?'

'Money, matches. I don't know what else.' He scoured the room for hiding places – under the bed, under the mattress, in her bedside cabinet, the en-suite cupboard. No luck. Then he walked over to the desk and unfolded the picture she'd just drawn. 'Gran, these drawings aren't doing you any good. Maybe you should stop.'

'I'll draw if I want.'

He took the drawing, folded it. 'I'll put this somewhere safe for you.'

'Why do you take everything away from me? It's mine. I'll keep it safe.'

He ignored her, put the folded drawing and the envelope full of money in his jacket pocket. 'You were at the back of the house last night, weren't you, Gran?'

'No!'

'You were. I know exactly where you are at any given moment. I can track you on my phone. Last night at 3 a.m. you were outside. At the back of the house.'

'How do you know that?'

'The tag, Gran, remember?' He lifted her jeans. The tag was still there, but it had marks on it. She'd obviously been trying to cut it off.

'You can't get it off. You must stop trying.' He turned to me: 'What's she been using to cut this? You let her have sharp implements?'

I hadn't given her the scissors as she'd asked. 'No. She must have found something. We don't let her—'

'Get out of my grandmother's room, and don't come back. Hear me? I don't want you to have anything to do with her again. You hear me, Gran? Do not talk to this girl. She's stealing from you. I want that money back, you hear? I'm going to complain to the owner. You should not be working here. If I catch you at it again, I'll call the police.'

Rose stood. 'Leave her alone. I can give money to anyone I want. It's mine.'

'Actually, Gran—'

She moved closer to him. 'Actually nothing, Christopher. You keep the money I gave you, Catherine, you hear me? I employed you. You earned it.'

She'd walked over to grasp my upper arms. I admit, I was a little scared of her, but not as scared as I was of Chris. 'You should go home. It's not safe here.'

'Gran, it's perfectly safe.' Chris was holding the Zimmer in front of her. 'Let's get some fresh air.'

*

I shut Mum's door behind me. Where had the trauma-less girl of a week ago gone? I was finding it difficult to breathe. I hadn't slept more than ten hours in days. I felt faint. How long since I'd eaten? Had I eaten anything since Mum moved in? I must have. But I couldn't remember eating, and I couldn't imagine ever wanting to again.

'Cath?'

Mum was awake. No, she'd seen me crying. The tears receded immediately. Amazing, that. 'Hey, Mum, you're awake!'

'You can't keep this up, darlin'.'

'Keep what up?'

'Twenty-four hours a day. You can't do this for ever.'

'It won't be for ever.' Shit! I hadn't just said that out loud, had I? Oh no, I had. 'I mean, it won't be. I won't.' There was no changing that sentence around.

'It's fine.' She laughed, held her hand out. 'Come here. It's fine. I've spoken to Marcus and we both agree you need time off. You've got to look after your own health, honey. For me? Take a couple of nights off, okay?'

I wanted to talk to her about what'd just happened. Whenever I made a mistake or felt guilty, she always listened and said the right things. Why did I ever think she was a crap mother? Because she hadn't baked cakes? What an areshole I am. I couldn't burden a dying woman with my pathetic selfish errors of judgement. 'But I don't want to leave you.'

She reached for a sheet of paper at the side of her bed. 'I made a copy of this for you.'

It was titled: 'The Brain Hospice – Symptom Time Line'. I started reading:

The question I am asked most often is How long? While the end stage path varies from person to per-

son, there do tend to be commonalities that can
help to 'see what we're seeing' and often, to esti-
mate how much time might remain.

Underneath were several sections.

3–6 weeks prior to death:

There was a list of symptoms:

increasing weakness on the affected side, falling due
to resistance to accept help, need for more assist-
ance with walking, confusion and memory loss,
increasingly tired etc. etc.

Mum had ticked all the things on that list.

2–3 weeks prior to death: If still walking, may
wander around the house a little, as if restless, more
urgency with urination, less interest in world at
large; more confused by choices – yes/no answers
are best.

She'd ticked three-quarters of the symptoms listed in
that section.
    I put it down. 'I don't want to look at this.'
    'Well it's helped me, knowing. I think it'll help you

too. Look, I'm not quite at the one-to-two-week stage, and I'm not at the five-to-seven-day stage, or the two-to-five, or the final forty-eight hours. Keep the list, so you know where we're at. You can go home and rest. I'll still be here when you get back.'

But she wouldn't be, not really.

*

On the way out, Rose pounced from behind her bedroom door. 'I drew it again.' She handed me the new drawing, and tried to give me another handful of money. Chris was right: she obviously had a hiding place in the room somewhere. Good on her. I wondered how much money was there. 'Please take it to Natalie. I don't know why I didn't think of her first. She's the one. She'll understand, even if I don't right now.'

'I'll take this to Natalie.' I put the cash in her palm, closed her bony fingers around it. 'But I won't take your money.'

As I was calling a taxi outside, Marcus drove up in his Merc, beeped, and wound down his window.

'Good, you're going home. You want a lift?'

The taxi number wasn't answering. I jumped in.

*

They say grief increases the libido, at least temporarily, something about the life-affirming nature of procreation. While I insisted on a non-procreating condom, I must agree about the life-affirming argument. I escaped grief for a moment (I'd say one minute, to be exact). For the other ten minutes or so I dreamt of taking a shower.

I'd invited Marcus in for a coffee and ended up giving him a whisky followed by a full-on kiss. While I was kissing him I was thinking to myself: this is wrong and selfish and – well, mainly wrong. Since Mum's bombshell I hadn't sought any of my usual pleasures at all – alcohol, humour, the Internet, friendships, food, or even a proper sleep. Apart from that half a joint, I s'pose, but that was medicine, to help me rest so I could resume my duties with competence. Yet here I was seeking out Marcus's thin and quite hard tongue, hoping it would relax, thicken and be less pointy if coaxed by my own tongue movements and enthusiasm. Alas, it remained pornstar pointy, prodding and twirling, unwilling to go back into his mouth or step inside mine: wriggle, wriggle, point, point, dab, dab. I should have stopped, but an urgency to disappear into flesh overwhelmed me. The thrust of tongue or body might yank the death out of me. I might forget for a moment. I might feel something other than fear.

So I kept going, leading Marcus into my bedroom, where I ordered him to lie down.

He asked me if I was sure about this and I told him to shut up.

He asked me if this was wrong, him being my boss and all, and I told him he wasn't my boss, he wasn't paying me, my mother was, so take your clothes off and shut up.

Marcus wasn't great naked. Despite a slim frame, he was soft and man-booby and his puffy knees were even puffier than I'd suspected.

I sat on top of him but he wasn't hard yet and this made me cry.

He told me to shut up this time, tossed me onto my back and began.

His moves were so slow and so gentle – like he was rowing a boat through a lake made of glue. Same movement, over and over. This was the worst sex I had ever had in my life, even worse than my first time: Derek Valien from my class at school. We were down in by the river in the Botanics and he came as soon as I touched him but he still tried to put it in me after because he didn't understand the logistics. As Marcus rowed his sluggish boat, moaning in unison with his oar, I found myself wishing for the quiet of grief. Let me think about my mother. Let me be with my mother.

I bounced on top and took over in order to get some anger in there. I wanted to punch him in the face as I began the grind. I wanted to yank his hair out till his scalp bled. I wanted to cut his head open with an axe and pull out his tumour-free brain and drive as fast as I could back to Mum, brain throbbing in my bloody hands, and pop it into her head. With knees like this, man-boobs like this, moves like these, he did not deserve a tumour-free brain.

'Stay still!'

I couldn't stop crying.

'Keep your eyes open.'

My tears stopped as I imagined strangling him with my hands, stomping on his stupid thin nostrils with my feet till his nose split in half.

We were vying for control. I was back under again, crying again.

'Stop wriggling!'

To get it over with, I stopped moving altogether while he stirred so quietly I could hardly tell it was happening. Finally, he shuddered a whites-of-eyes orgasm. I was glad he couldn't see the disgust on my face. Eeek!

I pulled myself out from under him and covered myself with the duvet. 'Thought I nearly lost you there.'

'Ah, yes.' He put his arms behind his head, triumphant. '*La petite mort*!'

'What?'

'The little death. Just what I needed, cheers.'

As I put my pants on, he raised his eyebrows: 'So, did you?'

I hated it when guys asked me this. If they had to ask, then they knew. And how could he even think that? I'd cried most of the time, and surely he'd noticed the murder on my face. I felt like torturing him. 'Did I what?'

'Did you die a little death?'

'Couldn't even conjure a fake one I'm afraid, Marcus.' But he was in danger of dying a big one if he didn't get the hell out of my house. I'm not sure you could call it kicking him out, but I do remember placing a firm hand on his lower back and encouraging him out the door. I should not have done that. It had not affirmed life. It had made it want to vomit. Why, why had I? Why hadn't I gone to Paul's house and hugged him? I rushed to my computer to write another email.

Subject: Life's too short and other clichés.

Paul,

I don't know what I've been waiting for. You should know how I feel. I want you to hold me and I don't want you to let go, ever. Well, you'll need to let go to go to the toilet and eat and get dressed . . . oh there's no getting away from it, you'll have to let go quite often, but you get the idea. I'm pressing Send this time.

I didn't give myself time to think. I pressed Send. Then I wrote another one.

> Subject: Please ignore previous email.
>
> Paul,
>
> Please ignore previous email. Please ignore previous email. Please ignore previous email.

*

I closed the laptop and jumped in the shower to scrub the ick from my body. There was something horrendous about Marcus Baird. Or was it just that it was a bad idea to douse grief with lust? No, he was revolting.

I put my favourite indoors outfit on – stripy PJ bottoms and sleeveless white T-shirt – and walked along the hall. I could see the study, to the left, with Mum's enormous desk, now cleared of all signs of life and work. I could see the bathroom, Mum's bedroom. I could see through to the dining kitchen leading out to our courtyard, laid out with stone slabs and low-maintenance shrubs and comfortable furniture that Mum could work on and I could bake myself on if it ever got hot enough. This was the home I'd grown up in. Since Mum chucked Martin Watson and bought it, I'd never thought about it much. It was just a house. Well, a ground-floor tenement flat. Would I sell it? If I did, it'd fetch a decent price. In the heart of Glasgow's West End. High, corniced ceilings, huge rooms. Magazine-stylish. My mum had done it up beautifully, and kept doing it up every year. A room a year, that was her rule. 'If you don't revamp a room a year, then before you know it, the house is run down, unpleasant to live in, and unsellable.' I can imagine that was on a list she wrote for herself when she moved into her first house: This, Maureen, is something I would like you to do from now on.

Her name's Maureen. Funny I've not mentioned that. Maureen Mann. And I'm Catherine Mann. You're a Mann, Catherine! You've got balls, my Mann? Thanks for the surname, Grandpa. Why my man-hating mother didn't take Martin's surname and give it to me for Christmas I never understood. Catherine Watson. Now there's a girl who wouldn't be bullied. Or my father's name: Catherine Marks. That's a girl who'd make a mark. Or something new, altogether, to be feminist about it. Like Chalmers. My name is Catherine Chalmers.

So this house was mine now. Just mine. Thanks, Maureen Mann.

I dropped to the floor of the hallway and cried into the recently repolished floorboards.

*

It was her clothes I went to first. Folk do that, don't they, gravitate to the garments that had last covered their loved one, hoping the Persil non-biological liquid had not wiped out their scent completely, that the flat arms of a jumper, the crumpled legs of a pair of jeans, might suddenly fill. Mum's wardrobe was always neat. A huge walk-in number that she'd had built one rainy November when she last revamped her bedroom. I shouldn't have been surprised when I switched on the light. All her clothes, and all her shoes, were gone. She hadn't even left me the things I stole regularly at that bloated time of the month – a windcheater from the Great Barrier Reef, a pair of yoga pants from H&M, a baggy blue T-shirt from I don't know where. I bet she considered keeping these things, but decided it'd just make things harder for me. She'd have imagined me agonising about throwing them out, being unable to, locking the room as a shrine, thereby wasting a very well-proportioned and brightly lit room that could house a gym set or a painting studio or a room-mate or a baby. The wardrobe smelt of bleach and carpet shampoo. I checked in the en suite, hoping for a half bottle of Chanel 19, or that lip liner I loved. There was nothing in the bathroom. Not even a toothbrush. As I went through the flat, I realised that my mother had wiped the scene of the crime. Her DNA was not to be found here.

In the study she'd left three photo albums, but had cleared everything else. She'd left a pile of envelopes, each labelled, containing copies of the documents I'd already seen at Dear Green.

The skip was still at the front of the flat. I jumped inside it, ripped at black bin bags, but none of her clothes were there, just papers and broken kitchen utensils, shit like that.

I grabbed Mum's keys, ran to her car, and drove too fast to our local Oxfam, crying all the way. I didn't know the shop assistant who approached me carefully and picked up some of the clothes I'd tossed to the floor, but she was quite kind about it, asking: 'Are you okay?'

'Do you know Maureen Mann?'

'Of course.'

'I'm her daughter. I think she brought some things here by mistake.' I realised I was in my PJs. I must've looked crazy.

The labelled boxes I'd seen in the hall last week were in the back of the shop, empty, the contents piled onto tables with other donations. The shop assistant, over fifty but not the usual twin-set type, assured me they hadn't been washed yet, and shut the door to give me privacy while I went through them.

Those grey trousers were hers. She wore them last time she went to London. The green T-shirt was hers. She wore that around the house all the time – slob wear.

Her Barrier Reef windcheater, her baggy blue tee – phew! I put it on over my T-shirt. One by one I identified her clothes, folded them, smelt them, linked them with a memory.

I gave the assistant all the cash in my wallet, and drove home to put my mother's clothes back where they belonged.

*

Paul was waiting on the step when I arrived home with a huge laundry bag of clothing in each hand. 'Sure-fire way to get someone to read your previous email?'

His smile looked a little guilty: he shouldn't feel so happy at a time like this. 'Please ignore previous email.'

I put the bags down by the door and sat beside him. 'Mum tried to give all her clothes away.' He put his arm around me, and pushed my head gently till it rested on his shoulder. 'This might have ended quite romantically if I wasn't going to tell you I had sex with a revolting creep before I sent that email.'

I could feel his shoulder stiffen a little. I lifted my head, waiting for a response. Eventually, it came. 'Have you showered?'

'For about an hour.'

He pushed my head back on his shoulder.

Paul helped me put the clothes back in Mum's wardrobe, then went to the kitchen to defrost some soup for me. I must have fallen asleep on the sofa before he brought it back. I woke mid-afternoon to find a note on the coffee table. (*Get some rest. I'll call you later, Love Pxxx.*) The telephone rang. 'Is Maureen there?'

'No.'

'Can you leave her a message? It's Davy, back from holidays. Just to say I can fix the tiling in the bathroom. Can you get her to call me?'

I hung up and went to the main bathroom. How annoying it must have been for her to leave a room imperfect. A tile had fallen off above the sink about three weeks ago. I touched the wall behind it. For the first time in her life, Mum had failed to complete all the things on her list. I loved it! I would never fix that tile.

There were a lot of missed calls on the landline. I scrolled through the numbers; it was obvious that people knew now. Her friends from work, her aunty in New Zealand, her best mate, Antonio, and a few of my old school friends, including Gina and Rebecca. Paul had left about ten messages from before today.

I got dressed, grabbed my bag and drove to Natalie's house. She didn't answer the door, so I poked my head over the side gate and spotted her reading on the back decking as her six-year-old jumped on the trampoline.

'Catherine! Come in. How are you?'

I hadn't told her about Mum, and cried when I did. 'Oh, you poor thing. That's just awful.' I didn't know Natalie at all, but when she hugged me I felt like I did. 'Is there anything I can do to help?'

'Well, I'm really thirsty.'

Home-made lemonade poured and iced, I gave her Rose's latest drawing, which she read with the same sad sigh as last time. The picture featured mangled faceless figures clambering around a bed in Room 7.

'She'd be much happier somewhere in the city. Could you talk to Chris about it? He won't even take my calls. Surely he could find somewhere else.'

When she asked how Rose was doing, I was surprised by my answers. Since we'd last spoken, she'd run away to the police, tried to phone them, her grandson had put an electronic tag on her ankle against her wishes, and her bedroom door had been locked from the outside so she couldn't get out.

'Electronic tag? Jesus! They locked her door? *Jesus!*'

'Mummy, can I watch *Dr Who*?' Wee Joey's jumping didn't ease as he spoke. He was the cutest boy I'd ever seen.

'Sure thing, my darlin'. Let me get you down from there.' Natalie unzipped the trampoline safety net, and helped him down. We followed him inside. Natalie switched on the TV and kissed him on his chubby cheek. 'The others will be back soon. Mind if I get some food organised? You would not believe how much these boys eat.'

I sat at the bench while she chopped onions. 'I can understand how frightening it is for relatives when a loved one wanders off, but what about consent? Even offenders have to agree to tags. I'd complain, but they wouldn't listen to me. Could you? It's not right.'

'Yeah, okay. I will. You're right, it's out of order, isn't it?'

I noticed some framed illustrations on the wall in the kitchen, all of a pretty little blonde girl doing normal things – eating strawberries, playing games, looking happy. I homed in, noticing something they all had in common. 'These look like Rose's?'

'Yeah, she drew them between the ages of ten and seventeen. They were never published.'

'She gave you them?'

Natalie nodded.

'Are they the originals? They'd be worth a fortune.'

'She gave me the originals, yeah, but I don't have them any more. These are copies. Long story.' Natalie wiped her eye – the onion, I supposed.

'Hey, Natalie, have you got the other two Kings and Queens ones she drew?'

Natalie fished them out of a box file on her bookshelf.

I scrutinised them beside the ones of Margie on the wall. 'Why does she put green wellies in all these pictures? She didn't do that in Tilly books, did she?'

Natalie stopped chopping onion, and put her hand on her mouth, shocked. 'Oh my God, I completely forgot. She told me about the wellies when she gave me the ones of Margie.'

'What about them?'

'If there are green wellies in her pictures, it means she was there, that it happened, that the picture is the truth. It was a kind of secret code she had, to help her remember Margie.'

I looked at the one of Beatrice. In the drawing of the room, there was a framed picture on the wall – inside the frame, a large pair of green wellies. 'So this picture means she saw someone putting lipstick on Beatrice.'

I looked at the next one. This time, the wellies were on the Queen's feet. The picture on the wall of the room was a map of Loch Lomond. 'Loch Lomond. Bonnie, bonnie banks.'

We both said it at the same time. 'Emma.'

'Which means she saw Emma in Room 7 as well? What does "Oh, so full of woe" mean?'

'Wednesdays child. Was Emma born on a Wednesday?'

'Don't know. She died on a Wednesday.'

'So what's the latest one about?'

I homed in on the figure on the bed. Small, bony, and – I hadn't noticed this the first time I saw it – with a black beanie, the Billabong label in beige lettering. 'Oh, that's Jason's hat, exactly. I think she's drawn the boy who just moved back in. Why has she drawn him? But there are no wellies, so it's not something she's seen.'

We put the three pictures on the bench, side by side. The only other thing they all had in common was the Queen and her bright red lips.

'I wonder if this is that nurse, what's her name?'

'Gabriella.'

'I know dementia patients suffer from paranoia, but do you think there's a chance something is going on there?'

I told her about the log entries for people who'd died, and how they had been written in a fountain pen – the kind Gabriella used; and then there was her attempt at euthanasia with her son.

'I'm going to do a bit of snooping. Brian might help.'

'Who?'

'My husband. He's in social work too. High up: wears suits. And I need to see Rose. You think you could take her for a walk along the river tomorrow afternoon, say at two? They wouldn't find out, I'd be careful.'

'Sure. If you park at the petrol station, you can take the path down to the river by the bridge. We'll meet you at the huge tree about fifty feet from the road, by the bend in the river. You'll see it.'

*

Back at home, I checked my mobile phone for the first time in days. One text from Marcus (*Thanks for that, smiley face, etc., etc.*). I deleted his text immediately, as it reminded me ... ew. There were twenty-eight from various school and college mates. A bunch of texts and missed calls from Paul. And a voicemail from Mum: 'Hey, Cath, I'm feeling good! Hope you're getting some rest. Just ringing 'cause I finally got hold of the tiler and he can fix that tile in the bathroom at three today, that's Wednesday. Just make sure you're there to let him in, yeah? His name's Davy. I've paid him already.'

I couldn't help but smile.

CHAPTER TWELVE

AGE 82

Oh, it was the weirdest thing. Not a feeling, an absence. Rose had enjoyed a few lengthy periods of lucidity recently, but this one was the best. She'd been at her desk for an hour, and she really felt like writing something new. That morning, she'd begged Gabriella to let her out of her room so she could use the computer in the activity room. With Gabriella keeping a ridiculously close eye on her, she searched sites and read posts in forums from people like her, or from carers of people like her. After being locked back in her room, she'd sat at her desk and tried to write about it. Her latest attempts at children's books were laughable. Perhaps she should start a blog. Tales of the demented! Good one. The pen was in her hand, but nothing was coming. She just couldn't describe it. It was ... She tried to think of something to compare it to, some feelings related to things she'd been through.

Not Margie's death, that was vivid as all hell. Not the news that her father was missing in action, which came two months after her mother collected her – and Margie's body – from the farm. Not the time her mother accused her of losing Margie's locket, the one she'd been given for her fifth birthday. Rose's mum and dad had spent half a month's wages on the locket, overwhelmed with joy that their sickly little girl had survived a near-fatal asthma attack. Inside the locket was a photo of her mum and dad. It was a beautiful photo, taken just before the war, when the girls were wee and there was nothing to worry about. Her dad was beaming in it, just like he did when he told Rose stories at bedtime. They'd told Margie to wear it around her neck always, to touch it and think of her parents when she was feeling unhappy or breathless, that the locket would keep her safe and calm and healthy and happy. When Rose's mum arrived at the farm, her baby girl was laid out on the dining room table, Violet the doll tucked beneath her crossed arms, but there was no locket around her neck. For the life of her, Rose could not remember when she'd last seen it. She felt implicated in its loss.

'Do you know where it is?' her mother asked. 'Please try and remember!'

Before leaving the farm to go home, Rose had scoured the farmhouse, the sheds, the riverbank. She'd even trawled the river with a colander. She'd questioned all the other children, certain that one of the little twerps had stolen it, recalling Margie saying that Bridget had taken it one night when she was sleeping, and Margie had to fight with her to get it back. But she couldn't find it, and she couldn't remember the last time she'd seen it, probably because she'd been self-absorbed at the time. Selfish, selfish girl.

There were so many feelings related to this experience, but none of them helped her write about this illness.

It wasn't a feeling, the disease, that's the thing. It was a lack of it. A lack of everything. It was like writing about a shapeless shadow.

She looked at the photos on her wall. There was Vernon at a restaurant table on his fortieth birthday. Such an old-fashioned name, Vernon. How she'd fancied that tall dapper man when they first met at the dancing in the East End of London. He spoke so little! Rose immediately assumed this was because his mind was overwhelmed with thoughts that were too complex and strange to share with others. He'd share them with her, she decided, and she'd understand. He half-smiled all the time, a witticism taking place in his head, no doubt, that she assumed was the same one she'd just thought. He intrigued and enticed her and she set about creating a story for him, writing his biography at night in bed, imagining him painting works of secret genius in his basement, explaining his philosophical views in university journals, making heartfelt and hilarious speeches at charity events. Vernon was the best character she ever wrote. And purely fictional. They married before she realised that his little smile was due to the shape of his lips, not a complex internal social commentary, and that his silence was because he couldn't think of a thing to say. They had two children together. He did his law degree in Glasgow and stayed there to become partner in a conveyancing firm. She was soon glad he didn't like talking much, especially about his work.

She wasn't glad when he died, aged fifty-two. He was a kind, hard-working family man. He provided and he spent time with the children. A week after his death, she was planting tulip bulbs in the garden. The sun was shining, and stories started filling her head. She'd done the wife-and-mother thing, perhaps to try and make up for her failure at the daughter-and-sister thing. She'd done well. But husband and children were gone now. She almost ran to the desk in the corner of the living room. She finished her first book in one month. Two months later, she had a three-book deal.

She'd met Vernon at seventeen, and stopped drawing pictures of Margie with wellie boots in them. Marriage, then motherhood, doused her grief and her guilt, and her father's last words didn't seem so important any more. She came to terms with what had happened. She was a good wife, a good mother, a good person and then, after Vernon died, she was a good writer. It was the dementia that brought her father's words back. He whispered them over and over as she wandered the maze.

The page in front of her was still empty. How could it be that she couldn't use this hiccup creatively? She'd always used everything that ever happened to her, no matter how awful. Being an evacuee. Losing a sister. That time the farmer fed them her favourite cow for Sunday dinner, and she knew the beef was Josie, but she was so hungry she ate anyway. She'd used childbirth, widowhood, even the coming out of her gay grandson (this particular plotline was vetoed, not surprisingly). But she couldn't use this, because she couldn't feel it.

Rose had often worried about getting arthritis, like the farmer's wife, whose hands had set in a gnarled knot. What if that happened to her? What if she couldn't draw? But arthritis would have been fine. She wouldn't have been able to draw, but she could have written, used an assistant, like the new girl, or dictated into a tape.

She looked on the wall for inspiration. There was Janey, her first born. So sullen and shy, like her father. So very serious. A millionaire now. There was Elena, happy with her partner in Canada and their two little girls. Rose would love to get on a plane and visit them again. And Chris, always here for her, bossy boots that he was.

Rose looked at the calendar on her wall, one of the devices the idiots in here used to keep her oriented. It was Thursday today.

Thursday morning! Oh, that's right. Thursday morning. She left the desk and stood at her window, waiting for the inevitable.

And it was only forty-five minutes before it came. When the trolley passed, the new girl unlocked her room, came in, and took her hand. 'Let's go and wave him off, Rose.'

Rose was beginning to like this girl. Tragedy had pummelled the dullness out of her. Rose took her hand and they watched Jason's body being rolled towards the ambulance. Just twenty-one. She'd achieved nothing at twenty-one, except killing her sister. She wondered if Jason had achieved anything.

She turned to Catherine as the ambulance drove off, his parents and his sister in the car behind. 'I remember now. That's what I was trying to tell you.'

'What?'

'That Jason would die.'

'Is that why you drew the picture of him in bed?'

'Yes, because he was going to die. I knew it. I was trying to stop it.'

'But we all knew he was going to die, Rose, even he knew. No one could stop it.'

'No, that's not what I meant at all.'

'What did you mean?'

'What?'

'What did you mean then?'

Rose leant in so close that she could feel the girl's breath on her cheek.

*

AGE 10

'Your breathing's getting worse, Margie.'

CHAPTER THIRTEEN

Two days without steroids and Mum had all but disappeared. She was sitting in her armchair, gazing at the female doctor like a newborn, eyes fixed in confused wonder.

'You must be Catherine.' No pause for confirmation or small talk before she continued her interrogation. 'I was just asking your mum if we've met before.'

Mum was supposed to understand this cue. She didn't.

'Have you met me before, Maureen?'

'Um, maybe we have.'

'And do you know who this is?'

The two seconds or so that followed seemed like an hour. The idea that my mother would not recognise me was unthinkable. I stopped breathing as she stared at me, her newborn face turning to a worried middle-aged one. She seemed as mortified as I was that she might get the answer wrong.

Then suddenly: 'Catherine.'

I could breathe again. 'Hey, Mum.'

'Good, that's good. Any pain in the head?'

Mum's hand was on her head now, clawing at her thick brown hair, a sure sign she was in agony.

'I don't think so.'

'Out of one to ten, how sore is your head?'

Mum bit her lip, as if she'd been asked to do an impossible calculus problem on the blackboard in front of the whole class. 'I don't know.'

'Okay, that's good, Maureen.' The doctor had a very slick outfit on underneath her coat. Tight skirt, heels. 'Make sure to say if you're in pain, won't you? We can give you something. I'll be back in a few days to check on you.'

I followed the doctor to the office and asked the things I should have asked as soon as I found out. Had my mother sought a second opinion? Yes, she'd had three separate consultations after the initial diagnosis.

'And there's really nothing?'

'Nothing.'

'Why did she refuse radiotherapy?'

'It was purely palliative. She didn't think another month was worth it, considering the side effects.'

'She has a symptom time line – is it about right?'

'I don't know which one, so it's difficult to say. You'll know when the time's coming.'

'How?'

'You just will. The staff here will too. There'll be a sudden downturn. When it's the brain, anything can happen. One thing at a time, or everything at once. She'll probably sleep more and more. Sometimes it can be quite gentle, a brain tumour. The blankness can take the fear away. She doesn't seem upset, which is good – personality changes can be a challenge, but that doesn't always happen.'

She gave me her contact details, and I went back in to see Mum. 'How you doing?'

'I'm tired.' She yawned. 'The cars kept me awake all night.'

'What cars?'

'Seemed like dozens of them, in the middle of the night, parking in the car park. Headlights and engines. I need to go to the toilet. Can you help me?'

The toilet trip didn't go well. Mum was shuffling with the Zimmer now. One tiny step after another. And she'd started humming when in transit: dum-de-dum-de-dum-de-dum. It wasn't a cute hum. A coping mechanism maybe, I don't know. I hoped the hum was temporary because it made me want to drop to the floor, curl into a ball, and stay there. She wasn't a whistler, hummer, or even singer. Not that she was dour, just that she had too many other things going on in her head to be consumed by meaningless tunes. She couldn't haul herself up to stand at the Zimmer afterwards.

It was 1.45 p.m. I tucked Mum in and went to the office, where I placed an envelope in today's logbook labelled 'For Rose's grandson, Chris.' Inside was £1,500 – what was left of the money Rose had given me topped up with some of the funds Mum had transferred to my bank account – and a note saying how sorry I was. It wasn't a hard note to write. I now felt terrible about taking Rose's money like that.

I turned the key to Rose's door. Surely it was wrong, illegal even, to lock her in? She was right, she was a prisoner. After talking to Natalie yesterday, I'd decided to talk to Marcus about the tag and the lock as soon as I got a chance. I tried to open the door, but it was stuck. I pushed harder, but the resistance increased.

'If I'm not allowed out, then no one's allowed in!' Rose was pushing from the other direction.

I stopped pushing. 'That's fair enough. It's Catherine, I won't come in if you don't want. I just wondered if you'd like to come for a walk? You fancy some fresh air?'

*

I shouldn't have picked the tree at the river bend as our secret meeting place. It sent Rose back in time. As Natalie and I talked, she raced around gathering twigs.

Rose placed the three twigs she'd managed to gather in a pile by the tree. 'Sit down, Margie! I'm going to get more wood.'

I did as Rose asked, my back against tree. She didn't

seem to notice that Natalie was there, that she sat down beside me, or that I was telling her about the boy who died last night.

'Was Gabriella on shift?'

'I don't know.'

'Can you do me a favour?' I don't know why Natalie whispered, there was no one around but Rose, and she was in another world, and time. 'Do you think you can get some time alone in the office?'

'I think I can; it depends how Mum is, mostly.'

'Sure, no worries if it's not possible, I understand and I hate to ask, with what you're going through. But if you do get a moment, can you take a photo or scan copies of those weird log entries you found? Here's my email address and mobile number.' She gave me her card.

'Okay, that's going to be nice and warm, Margie. You're going to be fine here till I get back.' Rose was pleased with the larger pieces of wood she'd found on the bank.

'And if possible, I'd like to know who has died here over the last six months and when – i.e. date, day, time. That's when she started doing those drawings.'

'You're scaring me, Natalie. Do you think I should get Mum out of there? What do you think's going on?'

'Can I trust you?'

'Of course.'

'Brian will lose his job if you tell anyone.'

'I promise.'

'When Gabriella's son was ill, they had social work input for a while – home help, occupational therapy, that kind of thing. She wasn't coping at all. After the Dignitas application was refused, the home help let herself in because she forgot her phone. Anyway, she found Gabriella sitting by her son's bed. She'd dressed him in his rugby kit, put his favourite music on, cooked his favourite meal, and was about to inject him with insulin.'

'He wasn't diabetic, was he?'

She shook her head. 'She denied it, and they couldn't prove it. But yeah, Brian and I think she was going to kill him.'

'Shit.'

'Email me the creepy log entries, the details of the deaths over the six months – longer if you can. And one more thing.'

'I'm just going to go to the kitchen and get some matches.' Rose was ready for the next stage of her trauma. The stealing of the matches.

'Can you get me Gabriella Nelson's shift pattern for the same period?'

'Holy shit, you think she's killing people!'

Rose returned to the present day before Natalie could answer. 'Natalie?'

'Hi there, Rose. How you doing?'

'You're not allowed here. You're a thief! You stole from me.'

'Rose, you know I—'

'I trusted you and you stole from me! Get out of my garden! Get off my land! You stopped visiting me! What sort of friend are you?' Rose was yelling and screaming so loudly that Nurse Gabriella heard and came running from the house.

'What are you doing here? We have an interdict, you're not allowed within two hundred yards of this place. Go now or I'll call the police.'

I looked at Natalie, who was shaking her head sadly. 'Is that true? You stole from her? Is that why you left your job?'

'You know how confused she gets, how easy it'd be to manipulate her.' She sighed. 'Honestly, though. All right, all right; I should just leave this. She's so unwell.' She turned and walked away, leaving me by the tree with Rose and Gabriella.

*

For the afternoon activity, they brought in a regular guest, a local author. H. R. Something. Jimmy was the only resident there, tapping, as usual, on his Samsung Galaxy. Nurse Gabriella and Marcus were listening in- tently as the author read a passage about a man tying a woman in a basement and torturing her. Odd choice! I'd been with Mum for the last hour, so I wasn't sure if they'd asked Rose if she wanted to go. I tapped on her door, unlocked it. 'It's Catherine, can I come in?'

'Sure, sure. Have a seat.'

'Did Natalie steal from you?'

'What?'

'Outside, you said Natalie stole from you.'

'Oh?'

'Yeah, by the tree, just now.'

'I was by the tree?'

No point badgering her, I thought. 'I wondered if you wanted to go the activity room? There's an author here.'

Her eyes lit up. 'Oh, who?'

'HR. I can't recall . . .'

'God, Henrietta Ruth. She's here all the time. I think she's milking us for material, frankly. No thanks, but I'd love to read a good book. Do you have a good book?'

'Not here, but I can bring one when I get a chance. For now I'll print something off for you to read. How does that sound?'

I nipped into the office, Googled how to pick a lock, printed off the first three articles, and handed them to Rose, who shook her head in confusion, then sat down to read them with the same look of intense concentration my mum always had when reading.

I closed Rose's door, but didn't lock it.

With everyone busy and elsewhere, I snuck into the office, locked the door, and grabbed the old logbooks with the moment-of-death entries, snapping them on my phone as quickly as I could before replacing them on the shelf. Even if Natalie was a thief, taking advantage of a vulnerable old lady, I needed to know if Gabriella was a murderer or – God – a serial killer.

I looked through the filing cabinet for the shift rotas that were printed each week, but they weren't there. I checked Word documents and spreadsheets on the PC, but couldn't find any file names that sounded right.

The rotas for the last eight weeks were pinned to the notice board, so I snapped photos of those. I heard a scratching noise. Was someone coming? No, it was Rose fiddling with her lock by the sound.

I froze for a moment to see if anyone else had heard. But if they had, they were ignoring it.

I leafed through the logbooks from the last six months, taking photos when a death was recorded.

Jason died yesterday, Thursday morning, it said.

Emma died last Wednesday.

The two before that died on Thursday.

Beatrice died six months ago, on a Wednesday.

The one before that, Wednesday.

In the last eighteen months, from when Carmel Tate died onwards, fifty per cent of the patients who died here, died late on Wednesday night. All the rest died very early Thursday morning.

I looked at my photos of the earlier logbooks, the ones with those strange entries about the moment of death. The patients who died more than eighteen months ago died randomly. There was no recurring pattern.

Someone was turning the door handle. I raced over and released the snib.

'Please do not lock this door again, Catherine.' It was Nurse Gabriella. She seemed terrifying to me now, with her dead son and her fountain pen and her lips so red.

'Okay, sorry.'

'Did you leave Rose's door unlocked?'

'Why? Did she get out?'

'No. She's busy reading. Did you forget to lock it, Catherine?'

'I must have. Sorry.'

She closed the office door and walked towards me, stopping when she was close enough to see my lips tremble. 'You let Natalie come here. She's not who you think she is, Catherine. She is not allowed to visit.'

'I didn't know that. But I think it's wrong how Rose is treated.'

'I'm sure you're young and arrogant enough to know everything about right and wrong. What was Natalie wanting?'

'Nothing, a visit, but Rose was confused, time travelling again.'

'Is she still giving her those pictures she draws?'

'I don't know.'

'Oh, I think you do.'

'And I think you're standing too close to me.' I bumped past her shoulder quite hard as I stormed out of the room.

*

Before Mum woke, I emailed Natalie the photos from my phone. She replied immediately.

'Cheers, Catherine. Could you come to mine tomorrow?'

'If Mum's okay here, sure, but you have some explaining to do.'

'I know. And I will explain.'

*

I kept busy that afternoon, reading articles from the *Guardian* to Mum that she seemed less interested in than I was, going through the three photo albums she'd left in the house, playing music, taking her to and from the loo, encouraging her to eat, asking if she was sore when she grabbed at her hair. 'I don't know,' she'd say.

I did a few of the jobs that Nurse Gabriella had identified as mine: scrubbed the kitchen, tidied the office, emptied the bin by the water cooler in the back corridor. I'd done the water cooler bin every working day since last Friday. Usually, there were around ten paper cups in the bin. Today there were twenty-five (I counted them). Someone had been thirsty last night. Maybe Jason's family, poor things.

Mum was dozing on and off most of the day. At ten o'clock, she looked settled, so I nipped upstairs. I was nervous Marcus might think we were an item after what happened yesterday evening. While the thought of being anywhere near him creeped me out, I needed to set the record straight.

*

As I said earlier, my relationships never lasted more than three months. Perhaps because underneath I already knew who I wanted to fall in love with, I never felt the need to try with anyone else, and I ran from it if I felt it coming. So I had developed many strategies to get rid of boyfriends when they showed signs of growing attachment. Sometimes a digital chucking would suffice – a simple un-friending on Facebook, coupled – if need be – by a blockage on Twitter and the non-answering of texts. If they knew friends of mine and/or where I lived, a contact chucking was required. I'd confront them – always in a public place so they couldn't get loud or tearful – and say, 'I just don't fancy you. I tried. I'm so sorry.' This worked well because there was nothing they could come back at me with. If I'd said, for example, that I was just coming out of a relationship, or that I was thinking about travelling, or that I had commitment issues, or that it wasn't them it was me, then there was room for negotiation. They could take it slow, no need to label it, no pressure, just fun (aren't we having fun?), or they could come travelling with me! My technique worked every time, and was usually true.

Marcus shut the laptop to take in my usual spiel. 'Look, last night was lovely, but I just don't fancy you.'

Men usually left in a huff after I said this. But I'd made a mistake. This was not a public place. It was his place. It could get loud, tearful and/or dangerous. Marcus sighed. He was going to get angry. He might ban me from the building. Or trap me here in his office. I checked the door was open and planned my escape.

'Thank God for that!' He laughed. 'I didn't want to hurt your feelings, but it just didn't work at all, did it? You cried the whole time!'

I faked a laugh. How dare he? My sexual prowess had never been questioned, ever. And especially when he was so grossly revolting!

'You were too gentle for me,' I held myself back from saying more.

'You were too frantic!' He flailed his arms. 'All over the place! Going this way, going that! What is that about, so aggressive? Are you always like that?'

We laughed together. Mine was even faker now. Okay, so I was peeved, and that made me want to put him in his place.

'You can have a nap on my bed.' He opened the lid of his laptop. 'I'm on a roll here!'

'What did Natalie steal from Rose?'

'That woman. Acts like some Mother Theresa, and all the while she's in it for the dosh. They found original artwork of Rose's in her house worth over nine thousand pounds. They should've locked her away.'

That's right, Natalie had some illustrations in her kitchen. She said she used to have originals, but now only had copies. 'She told me Rose gave them to her.'

'Rose was the one who phoned the police!'

Wow, so Marcus had good reason to ban Natalie from visiting. Maybe all the restrictions they put on Rose were for her own protection. But Gabriella still worried me. 'I have a confession. I don't like Nurse Gabriella. I don't trust her. When I ask her a question, she never gives me a proper answer, as if she's keeping something from me.'

'Ach, she's just unhappy. Poor thing. Her son died.'

'Yeah, I know, but do you think she could be crazy; dangerous?'

'I think most people could be. Y'know, Rose isn't all sweetness and light, either. The bizarre stuff she comes out with, I don't think it's all the illness. I think she likes to wind people up.'

'What do you mean?'

'Just that I wouldn't take her too seriously, with the stuff she goes on about. She's very ill, but she was a shit stirrer before, apparently, and very self-centred.'

'Who says?'

'Chris. And he loves her.'

I didn't want to bitch about Rose. It seemed wrong, so I changed the subject. 'Tell me about your novel.'

'I'll let you read it when I'm finished.'

'Can't I just read what you've done? Maybe it'd help to talk about it.'

'I don't need to talk about it.'

'What's it about?'

He started typing, didn't want to talk. I kept talking.

'What's the title?'

'Not sure yet.'

'Go on, let me read a bit. Or tell me the synopsis.'

He exhaled and shut the lid again. 'It's hard to describe.'

'Try.'

'You can't really say what it's about. The character

is searching.' As was Marcus, for words to describe his work of utter crap.

'You said you had to Google weird shit. Is it crime?'

'Oh, well yes and no, hard to categorise, which is totally what I'm aiming for. I don't think there's anything quite like it out there. If there was a gun against my head and I had to label it – literary mystery, perhaps? But it's not about a crime, although there is one, it's about . . . it's about the things I feel I must say.'

I yawned, wishing I did have a gun at his head, and then I spotted a blue felt box on his desk. It was open, and it had a fountain pen in it. This place was fountain pen central! 'Actually, I don't need to read it. Doesn't sound like my kind of thing. I don't think I'd like it.'

I popped into his super-kingsize bed with satin sheets and duck-feather duvet, and slept for three hours.

He was asleep on the leather sofa in the office when I woke. The laptop was still open.

His book did have a title: *The Little Death*. A page was enough for me to see that Marcus was about as deep as a blackhead. In fact, it read exactly like the passages the detective fiction author read in group activity the other day. A cop with a past discovering a whole heap of fucked-up dark shit.

It wasn't possible to stop there. I checked his Facebook page – 378 friends, most of them his age and into music. Nothing saucy in his messages.

I couldn't open his email account, bummer. So I looked through his photos. The ones on Facebook were mostly party shots – groups of well-dressed young things with posh beers in their moisturised hands.

I don't know what made me remember the jpeg number I'd seen listed in the logbook, but as soon as I saw that he had hundreds of unnamed pics in 'My Pictures' it sprang to mind. 145. I clicked on it.

Holy shit, the photo was of close up of an elderly woman's face. What was her name? Bridget or something.

She died in Room 3, in bed, window closed. She was alone . . . She sat bolt upright and took a last silent breath. She looked excited, as if she could see someone at the end of the bed.

Her last words: 'You're there!'

At the moment of death, there was small rectangular shape reflected in her left eye (145.jpeg)

I zoomed in on her left eye. A white light, rectangular. Probably from the strip light above her bed. I closed the photo and all the other tabs I'd opened.

The A4 notepad on his desk was filled with chapter outlines. His writing was neat, but not in capitals like in the logbook. All in the black ink of his fountain pen. Considering the jpeg I just found, it was probably

Marcus – not Gabriella – who wrote those death entries in the logbook. Research for his book, perhaps. God, everyone here was so fucking weird. No wonder, I supposed. Spending days with the dying was already making me exhausted and paranoid.

'What are you doing?'

I had no time to move away from his desk, no time to lie. 'Oh, I'm sorry, I just couldn't sleep. I started reading your novel and I couldn't stop. It's compulsive!'

Marcus pounced down towards the laptop and grabbed it. 'First you take money from Rose.'

'Chris told you?'

'Rose told me. Now you snoop through my things. Your behaviour is completely unprofessional.'

'I'm sorry, Marcus. I just needed a distraction. It's my mum.' I was faking the tears, and felt guilty about it, but it was the only way out that I could think of. How awful would it be, to be kicked out of this house now, with my mother still aware enough to realise. I sobbed, moved closer to him.

He put his arms around me, reluctantly. 'I know.'

'You won't ban me, will you?' I paused, sob, sob. 'You're such a good writer, Marcus. You're going to be famous one day.'

His embrace tightened. 'You really think so?'

*

When I went back downstairs, my mother, Maureen Mann, a director of Oxfam and of me, and maker of lists, and doer of things, was on her stomach on the bedroom floor, clawing at the carpet in an attempt to get to the toilet.

She stared at me, perplexed. 'I can't seem to get up.'

I thought I'd be able to get her up by myself, like last time in the bathroom, but I ended up stuck underneath her torso, both of us unable to move. I was rough in the process. She'd probably have bruises under her arms tomorrow. I yelled and Nurse Gabriella came immediately, using well-practised techniques to get her to a kneeling position, and then onto the bed.

So coming off the steroids hadn't improved her mobility. It would deteriorate regardless.

That day, the rails went up on her bed, the Zimmer was replaced with a wheelchair, commode and sponges replaced the bathroom, and an emergency alarm she did not seem to understand – and would never use – was placed on a ribbon round her neck. A slow-moving hoist was installed beside the jail-bed to help her sit up to eat. The occupational therapist showed us how it worked. If used properly, Mum would be sitting up, ready to eat, in an agonising fifteen minutes. I watched as she had seizure after seizure, not violent as I would have imagined, just her arms shaking a little beyond a shiver, a scary-blank stare following for minutes afterwards. I was watching my mother be murdered by a serial killer; one the divorced, alcoholic detective would never catch.

That evening, when she finally slipped into a fretful sleep, kicking legs that refused to move when she was awake, I went into the office, shut the door, and cried. Rose must have heard me from her room next door. She knocked quietly before coming in.

'Rose, how did you get out of your room? Did you learn how to pick the lock?'

She held up a hairgrip, then put it in her hair. 'That one, my dear, is a gigantic piss-piece. When I grow up, I'm going to be a cat burglar.'

'You know I didn't steal from you, don't you?'

'Of course.'

'And Natalie, she didn't steal from you, did she?' A blankness moved over Rose like a shadow. I wouldn't get an answer to this question.

CHAPTER FOURTEEN

AGE 10

Margie was sobbing, the blossom. Trying to get air for so long had made her upset. She was giving up, Rose knew it. 'I'll go for help. Stop the tears, breathe. You stay here.'

'Come back, Rose, come back. It's me, Catherine.'

'Shhh. I will come back! I'll be so quick and then we'll sneak some cake from the pantry!'

Margie sighed. 'Look, look at my name tag. See, it says Catherine.'

'Why are you wearing that?'

'You were here a moment ago. I need you. Please.'

'I promise. I swear I'll be back. Just stay where you are and keep calm, keep breathing. I'm going to get some matches from the farmer's kitchen.'

The farmer had a name, but Rose didn't like to use it. He was a mean man and he didn't deserve a name. Rose and Margie and the others worked ten hours a day. The meals were tiny and tasteless and cold more often than not. Their beds were lumpy, their room an ice-box. He rarely spoke and he never listened. Once, Rose had gone into the wife's room to beg for mercy on behalf of all the children. She was tiny, withered, all curled up in her un-lumpy bed. Rose didn't have the heart to add to her problems. 'Sorry,' she said instead. 'Wrong room.'

'Wait! Let me show you something.' Margie ran off. If she could do that, maybe she was getting better.

She was back again, so quick!

'Look at these. You're an author, aren't you, Rose? Look at these books. You wrote all these books.'

Rose studied the girl at the office door, red-eyed, blonde, books in hand. Apricot shirt, name badge, a little girl, but not seven.

*

AGE 82

'A first draft always took me three months. That's quite quick, I believe. People always asked me about discipline. I always said: I have to discipline myself to not write.'

The girl put her in bed and started reading her a Tilly book, the one about the roast dinner. As always, there were elements of reality in the story. In the real-life version, the farmer had served roast beef and all the trimmings to celebrate the news that his eldest son, missing in action, had been found – injured, but alive. For the first time in months, they had enough to eat. But Rose knew the meat was her favourite Jersey, Josie. Why else had she disappeared from the south field the day before? Rose tried not to eat, and couldn't stop herself, but cried through the mouthfuls.

In the Tilly version, Rose's young heroine knew the farmer's Sunday-lunch plans, snuck out of the house in the middle of the night, and led Josie four miles to safety, leaving her to live a long, happy life in the pasture of a kind neighbour.

The girl had finished the story. 'I like it when you're eighty-two, Rose.'

'What?'

'When you're yourself. Do you know quite often you go back to when you were ten, to when you were trying to save Margie? You run through the same sequence, again and again. Did you know that?'

'Oh yes, I think someone told me that.'

'You run off to the river, run back and steal matches, light a fire. It's not nice for you, going back to what happened with Margie all the time.'

The dementia had brought this memory back and blown it up so large that it obliterated all others. 'I should have stayed with her. I should have stayed and sang her the song while she died. I know that's what she wanted.'

'What song?'

'"Imagination." I used to sing it to her every night.

She loved it. If only I'd stayed with her.'

'Keep talking. If we talk about it, it might stop it happening.'

'I wonder if they've tried that. I don't know. Can you get that box in the corner?'

Catherine opened the box file Rose had pointed out. Inside were black-and-white photos of the farm. It was a small ramshackle house, no more than three bedrooms by the looks. One of the photos showed the attic, a bare-looking dormitory with half a dozen scabby mattresses on the floor. Six children stood, gathered at the window with miserable, hungry faces, like something out of *Oliver*.

'Is that you?'

Rose was so angry in that shot. She didn't want the farmer in the children's room. She didn't want her picture taken. Her scowling ability was already legendary. 'Yes. And that's Margie holding the wee doll . . . oh, Margie. Can you hand me that doll on the shelf?'

The girl handed her Margie's doll, a Christmas present from her parents. Rose got one of these dolls too, but she lost it playing fairies at the canal a few blocks from their London home. Margie had never let her doll out of her sight. 'She wanted to call her Ro-Ro after me, but I told her she was too pretty for that. Her name's Violet.'

'I bet Margie just fell asleep at the tree. I bet she

understood why you left to get the doctor and she fell asleep feeling positive, with hope. You were a good sister. Margie loved you.'

'I suppose she did. She shouldn't have. She shouldn't have! She shouldn't have loved me!' All of a sudden, Rose felt like smashing things.

*

AGE 10

Oh how she wanted to smash things. And she would! The thing in her hand, she'd smash it against the wall. 'You're a selfish girl, Rose Price! You're a selfish, selfish girl, Rose Price!'

Someone was yelling at her – was that Margie yelling? 'Rose, stop it! Rose, don't, please; Violet, you'll break her.'

Someone was grabbing the thing in her hand.

Someone was sad. 'Oh no, oh no, Rose, but don't worry, I'll fix her. I'll fix her. That's it, into bed, close your eyes, everything's okay, Rose; everything's just fine, lie down there now, beautiful, unselfish Rose Price.'

CHAPTER FIFTEEN

The doll wasn't really broken, as I'd thought. The head had come off, but it had obviously been taken off once before. I knew this because someone had stuck a plaster to the inside of the skull. The plaster was yellow, ancient, and came unstuck easily. Something fell into the body of the doll. I turned Violet upside down and shook. A silver locket on a delicate chain fell out. Inside was a photograph of a very good-looking young couple. The man had such kind eyes, and an infectious, easy smile. I pushed the doll's head back firmly in place. Violet looked perfect again. Oh, Rose would be so pleased.

Mum had her eyes closed, and was picking at her clothes as if she were covered in flies. When she opened them, she stared at me for at least a minute before she understood where she was, who I was. 'Did the tiler come?'

'Yep, it's all sorted.'

She sighed, relieved, then resumed picking at her clothes.

Mum had just said something completely lucid and succinct and important (to her). It was completely

Mum. 'Did the tiler come?' A question, which had an answer, which I was able to give, and it soothed her. A moment later, however, this is what she said: 'I can't believe I'm back in this house again. It seems amazing. With all this furniture! Where did all the furniture come from?'

What did Mum mean about the furniture, I wondered. 'Have you been in this house before?'

Mum didn't answer. She was looking at the bedside table in wonder, touching it, shaking her head. 'After all this time! It seems incredible!'

'What's incredible about it?'

Mum thought hard about my question. 'I don't know.'

To this day, I have no idea where she thought she was – at her parents' house, maybe? Oh, I'd love to know. Wherever it was, she was happy there. Whatever it was, it was as real to her as the tiler fixing the tile in the bathroom of our house.

*

When I unlocked Rose's door, she was sitting at her desk writing. Phew, eighty-two. 'You have a good rest?'

She looked up from the page she was working on. Just words so far, by the looks. No picture. 'Did I have a rest? I have no idea. I can't describe this illness, Catherine. I can't find any way to describe it.'

'Don't, then.' I put the doll on top of the page that was frustrating her. 'I fixed Violet.'

Rose touched the doll and smiled at it.

'Oh, did you want this to stay inside her still? It's not too hard to get the head off and on again.' I handed her the locket.

She stood, not breathing, lifted it gently from my hand, opened it, and fell back into her chair. 'Where did you find this?'

'Stuck to the inside of Violet's head with an old plaster.'

Rose began sobbing.

'What? What is it, Rose?'

'Margie, she must have hidden it there . . . From that little bitch, what was her name again? Look at him, look at my dad. Isn't he beautiful? Doesn't he look like the most loving and lovable person in the whole wide world?'

I told her he did. I wasn't humouring her.

'What do think he's thinking in this photo?'

'Happy things. He's thinking happy things, Rose. That's a smize! Smiling with his eyes. Impossible to pretend, unless you're Tyra Banks.'

'So he's not thinking that I'm selfish.'

'No, he's thinking he loves you.'

Rose stood by the mirror, and placed the chain around her neck. 'Will you fasten it for me, please?'

Once secured, she beamed at her reflection. 'Will you promise me something?'

'Of course.'

'Promise me no one will ever take this off me?'

I extended my pinky and this time Rose understood, and curled her own around mine. 'Pinky promise.'

*

It wasn't unusual to hear terrifying and upsetting noises in this place: screams of pain, yells of anger or frustration, cries of grief. Someone was crying. I left Rose to drink in her long-lost locket and ducked into the hall to check where it was coming from: Jason's parents; collecting his belongings.

'They're sad they missed him,' Nurse Gabriella said later.

'They didn't get here in time?'

'No, not till morning, I'm afraid.' The witch was softening, it seemed. Maybe the red lips in Rose's picture were not hers.

'So who drank all that water last night, then?'

'What?'

'The bin by the water cooler was full of cups this morning. I'd emptied it yesterday.'

She hardened again – 'How would I know? I never do Wednesdays.'

'Oh? Why not?'

'Not that it's any of your business, but since my boy died, I've stayed with Mum in Rothesay Wednesdays.'

'You're close to your mum?'

'She's my rock.' Her eyes welled. I'd never seen this side of her before.

'You get the ferry?'

'No, I swim.' And soft Gabriella morphed back into the bitch I knew.

A bitch who did not kill people here.

*

At midnight, the only other member of staff was old Harriet, who was sneaking a nap in Jason's ex-room. I wondered about the cups in the water cooler. There must have been other people here last night. I also re-membered Mum's comment – that cars had kept her awake all last night – and wondered if there were CCTV tapes. I'd noticed cameras at the front and at the back of the house but I couldn't find any tapes in the office. When Harriet woke, I asked her.

'Oh, Marcus doesn't believe this place should feel like a police state. We haven't used the cameras for well over a year.'

Odd, I'd have thought security was essential at a place like this.

'How long have you been working here?' I followed her to the kitchen, where she put some bread in the toaster.

'Since the beginning of time!' She laughed, getting jam and butter out of the industrial-sized fridge. 'Ten, no, eleven years.'

The toast was burning. Harriet turned it off in a panic, opened the window, waved a towel at the smoke detector on the ceiling. 'Watch this toaster. It sets that thing off all the time, and if the alarm goes off the fire engines arrive within minutes.'

She'd averted the crisis, stopped waving the towel.

'Okay. When did Marcus take over?'

'Two years ago.'

'And how long has Gabriella been here?'

'Five years. She and I are the only ones that stayed on.'

There was a garage about twenty metres from the end of the drive. I offered to get Harriet some chocolate, and headed out for some air. Opposite the drive was a mirror on a tall pole, so drivers exiting here could see if cars were coming along the windy main road. As I was buying the chocolate, I noticed the CCTV video on the wall, showing shots of the pumps and the cash machine. In one view, you could see the mirror opposite Dear Green's driveway.

'You work at the care home?' The young guy in the garage looked bored and tired and easily chat-up-able.

'Kind of. Needed a break. It's nice to see a young face.'
I pressed my arms together and leant in to give him a
shot of my cleavage.

A few minutes later, Greg was showing me the
CCTV tapes from last night. He fast forwarded from
10 p.m. onwards. One car drove in at eleven. One left at
eleven ten. Shift change, probably. Nurse Gabriella leaving, Harriet arriving. No cars at all for three hours after
that, then all of a sudden, car after car after car. Eleven
in total, all arriving between 2.20 and 3 a.m. I couldn't
see any of the passengers or number plates, just the headlights in the mirror as the vehicles turned into the drive.
No coming and going after that until half past five, when
all eleven cars exited in convoy.

I promised Greg we'd have a drink soon, then walked
back to Dear Green thinking about the cars. Where was
Marcus last night? We'd had a drink in the evening,
gone home, had terrible sex. Yes, he would have been at
home after midnight. Oh, perhaps he'd had a party. Of
course.

*

I went upstairs to his straight away. He was at his desk,
tapping away at that shit book of his. 'Hey, Marcus, just
wondering... Mum said lots of cars were coming and
going late last night?'

'She did?' Fearing I'd steal his ideas, he slapped the lid shut and turned his attention to me with a huff. 'The confusion's very difficult, isn't it?'

I didn't want to confront him and tell him I'd been looking at CCTV footage. It'd seem odd, me snooping about like that, especially after the complaint Rose had made, and me looking through his laptop. Instead I said: 'So there were no cars?'

'Not that I know of. Shift change at eleven last night. Jason's family arrived around seven this morning, I think.'

'So what did you get up to last night?'

'After yours? Sleep! Does she know who you are still? Does she need the doctor, you think?'

'No. I mean yes and no. I'd better get back to her though.'

So, either Marcus was a liar, or another member of staff had people over last night and he hadn't heard the cars. I hadn't decided which option to believe before I arrived back in Mum's room.

She looked so ill that I stopped wondering about paper cups and cars coming and going and Marcus lying (or not) and Natalie stealing and investigating shift patterns and logbooks. I didn't go home, I didn't visit Natalie as I'd promised, I didn't go next door to see Rose, or to the dining room, or the activity room, or the office, or upstairs to Marcus's flat, or to the garage. I sat in the armchair and held her hand. I gave her a sponge bath, told her stories, played her music, talked about her mum and dad, her childhood, showed her photos.

The three albums she'd kept were all about us, me and Mum. Only a few photos were from before I existed – of her fishing with her dad up north somewhere, of her and both parents at the fair in Glasgow. Then me as a new-born in hospital. Mum, despite the horror story of my birth, looked happier than I'd ever seen her, looking into my eyes the way new mothers do, in love. Her pushing me on the swing in that wee park in Dowanhill. Us in raincoats on a ferry to one of the islands. Us having fun, laughing.

Paul visited at some point. He brought a mixed CD he thought Mum would like, and a basket of food for me. I cried for a while in his car. 'I'm sorry, you're in the middle of exams, this is the last thing you need.'

He held my hand and put on the face that used to make me jump up from couches, run a mile. 'You do know I feel the same as you, don't you?'

I'm only going to give you one word to describe the kiss. Actually, no I'm not. Not a one.

'Call me when you need me,' he said after. 'Now get out of my car!'

Antonio visited twice. I heard him tell Mum he loved her. She said, 'Quite right.' He laughed.

There was a lot of love going around.

Gina and Rebecca phoned to ask how I was, then talked for a lot longer about how they were.

Therapists came and went.

Catheter came, never went.

I took Mum for a walk in the wheelchair a few times, the process of hoisting her from bed to chair and back again so exhausting and pointless that I stopped thinking it a grand idea by Monday.

There were no conversations any more. She understood me sometimes, and answered yes and no to food or drink, but rarely more than that. So it was a shock when she interrupted the story I was reading and said: 'You were never a mistake.'

'What?' She hadn't looked at me this way since she came off the steroids. She was actually seeing me.

'You always thought you were a mistake when in fact you were my great achievement.'

I burst into tears, ran over and hugged her. 'Oh, Mum. I love you. I love you so much.'

She pushed me off. 'What's all that noise?'

I could only hear Paul's CD playing quietly in the corner. Tracy Chapman, it was. Her favourite. 'You mean the music?'

'That's not music, is it?'

No music after that. All noise was noise, and it pained her.

I read the time line on the table beside her bed. She'd

ticked all the symptoms on the two-to-three-week stage, but had stopped ticking after that, like she'd stopped walking and making sense and lifting a fork to her mouth.

I looked at the one-to-two-week stage:

Often, completely bedridden

May find loud or multiple sounds irritating

After waking, seems confused for several minutes

Staring across the room, up toward the ceiling or 'through' you

May look at TV but seem not to be watching it.

I ripped the time line into tiny pieces.

CHAPTER SIXTEEN

By Wednesday afternoon, Mum had been sleeping for
eighteen hours. We'd managed to wake her a couple of
times to get a drop or two of soup into her mouth.
At 5 p.m. I was putting a clean sponge of water to her
mouth when Nurse Gabriella called me into the office.
'Your mum left me instructions, Catherine. She asked
that you go and stay with Antonio now for a couple of
days. He's coming to collect you in an hour. You do understand?'

I did. I wished I didn't.

'I don't know what I'd do if I were you. Do you want
to talk about it?'

'Aren't you supposed to be in Rothesay?'

'I'm going now. I wanted to say goodbye to your
mum. She's an incredible woman, Catherine. I'm so
sorry.'

*

Oh, Mum, wake up and give me a list! I'll squeeze the
toothpaste to the top and roll up the tube and close

the lid. I'll put the recycling bin out and I'll turn the lights off when I leave a room and I'll read a non-fiction book and two things out of every three that I say to you will be positive and this, Mum, is something I would like to do from now on. Wake up and give me a list. I'll do everything on it. You can check my progress next Sunday, give me a disappointing treat.

But she wouldn't be around next Sunday. And she'd already given me a list. The death plan.

*

Marcus was talking on the phone when he let me in. 'Okay, right, I'll have to call you back.' He hung up.

'Just came to tell you I'm leaving today.'

'Oh, Catherine, I'm so sorry.'

'Do you promise she won't be in pain?'

'I promise.'

'And you'll call me when it happens?'

'I will. Will you be okay?' His phone rang – a loud and intensely irritating train whistle. 'Where are you going?'

The train was still whistling, he hadn't pressed Ignore. 'Take the call, Marcus. I'm off. I'll be fine.'

*

My phone buzzed as I approached the back door. Natalie didn't even say hello. She sounded frantic. 'Did you see that long number thing at the bottom of the entry from eighteen months ago? The woman's name was Carmel Tate, died on a Wednesday?'

'No. Look I can't talk just now. It's really not a good time.'

'I'll text it to you. Looks like a code. If you get time to have a look, maybe you'd know if it's something innocent, like for the alarm system or a bank account?'

'Natalie, please. I can't talk.'

'But I need to tell you. I think Rose is on to something. All the drawings she sent me, they all tie in with the deaths there, exactly. The details in each one are right.'

'But that doesn't mean anything. Those people did die while Rose was here. I have to go.'

She wasn't listening to me. 'Gabriella's not the one. She's never worked those nights, not a once, which is weird, don't you think? They must keep her away. She's not involved.'

'I know Gabriella didn't kill anyone! No one did, Natalie. Rose is sick and you're a thief and a liar and a busybody and Dear Green is a hospice where people die. It's happening right now, to Mum.'

'But listen to this. Jim Thornton is a sex offender. He did twelve months back in 1985.'

I was shocked and didn't know what to say at first. *But then*, I thought, *so what?* Sex offenders get old and have to live somewhere. Mass euthanasia, or whatever Natalie was currently suspecting, would hardly be the MO on an elderly paedophile. 'That's a long time ago, Natalie.'

'But he and Marcus knew each other before he moved in!'

Okay, so this was slightly more interesting. 'How?'

'They were in the same poetry group.'

Maybe Jimmy was at the group to work on lyrics – he was a musician, after all. I was beginning to suspect that Natalie was far more confused than Rose. 'Natalie, I'm going to hang up now. Can you leave this, it's crazy. I trust you less than anyone right now, to be honest.'

'I have to get to work – doing some agency stuff to make ends meet. I'll text you the code, though; just take a look. I think it's some kind of password or something. Who has a computer there?'

I was getting annoyed at her now. 'Natalie, I don't want to hang up on you, but . . .'

'Just quickly, what computers?'

'There's a PC in the activity room. Jim has a smart phone. Marcus has a phone and a laptop.'

'Where's his laptop?'

'Upstairs.'

'Where?'

'He had it in his office last I saw, but it's a laptop, Natalie. It's portable.'

'Thanks, Catherine. Stay with your mum. I'll be in touch in an hour or so.'

'Don't . . .' I was going to tell her not to get in touch for several days, or ever, but she'd hung up.

*

I'd like to say my goodbye to Mum was a moving, beautiful, and satisfying closure. I'd like to say we hugged and cried together, that I told her I was sorry for being ungrateful, selfish and lazy; that I admired and respected her more than anyone in the world. I'd like to say that she understood.

But she was still asleep. I didn't say anything. I kissed her forehead, then her cheek, whispered, 'Bye, Mum, I love you,' and left.

*

Chris saw me in the car park, crying so hard I couldn't start the engine. He got in the passenger side without asking.

'Gabriella told me. I'm sorry.'

I couldn't talk through the sobs. Chris leaned over, held me. 'Where are you going?'

'She wanted me to be with Antonio, but I want to be by myself, I think. I don't want to leave. Will she be okay here?'

'Of course she will.'

'Did you know Jimmy's a paedophile?'

Chris looked bewildered. 'Have you been playing Inspector Morse?'

'Not me, Natalie.'

'Rose's Natalie?'

'Aye.'

Chris sighed loudly, as if he wasn't surprised. 'Natalie Holland is mad. She's always wound Gran up like you wouldn't believe. She stole nearly ten grand. Now she spends her time getting paranoid. Listen, I do know about Jimmy. You think I didn't take a good look at this place before letting Gran move in? Could have got me sacked, snooping around police records, but I would never have put her here if I didn't know for sure it wasn't the best and the safest place around. Jimmy has a record, yeah, but way, way back. He did his time, even did the treatment programme. And he's not a paedophile, by the way. Your mum will be well looked after here.'

'But . . .'

'You're flipping out. I don't blame you. But this is what she wanted. Was she comfortable when you left her?'

'Yes.'

'Were the staff looking after her?'

'Gabriella's leaving soon, then Harriet. The doctor's coming to sort out the morphine. Yes, okay, yes, they are.'

'Then do the right thing, Catherine. Do what she wanted, or you'll regret it.'

*

I drove. At first I didn't know where, just grabbed the A82 and headed north, like Mum and I used to do sometimes. 'Just get in!' she'd say. We'd be out of Glasgow in twenty minutes, Loch Lomond on our right till we decided where was best for lunch. Loch Fyne usually, for delicious seafood. Or further north if we fancied an island hop, or a walk.

My phone beeped several times after I'd been driving an hour and a half. I stopped at the side of the road and read the messages from Antonio. He was in a panic. *Sorry Ants*, I replied. *I need to be alone. I'm okay. I hope you are. I'll call soon. xxxx.* As I pressed Send, Natalie phoned.

'Catherine, Catherine.' She was whispering, and the signal was poor, in and out. 'I have an idea . . . upstairs . . . Did you . . . text . . . the code . . .'

'You're breaking up. I can't hear you.'

'I'm going to break . . . the next day or so, if he goes out. Don't leave . . . that . . .'

Just crackles after that. I spoke loudly and firmly. 'Please stop calling me, Natalie. And maybe you should think about getting some help.'

I kept driving north. It was 6 p.m. now. How long had Mum been in that 'final forty-eight hours' stage? She hadn't woken all day, hadn't eaten since last night, and when I left, she'd started making those horrible gurgling noises. She could be gone already. Or she could have another day or two.

I had to drive as far as I could so I couldn't turn round and be back in time. After all the things I'd done to disappoint her over the years, I had to do this one thing. I kept on the A82, past Crianlarich, along the A85 towards Oban, where there were ferries.

We went to Iona together once. Jumped on the ferry to Mull, then again to Iona, where we walked for a while before realising we were starving. There was nowhere to eat. It was hours before we made it back to Oban, to stuff our faces in the first restaurant we could find.

The 8 p.m. to Mull would leave in twenty minutes. With my car in the queue to go on, I remembered the fun we'd had when we came here last, and the fun we had so many times. 'Just get in the car!' And we'd be off. Not planned, not on a list.

Mum wasn't all about lists.

The ferry had come in, the ramp was coming down. If I took this ferry, I wouldn't be able to get back tonight.

I remembered her birth plan. She hadn't wanted drugs. She hadn't wanted to go to hospital. Then the pain came. And she regretted it.

I remembered her asking me what to wear to some charity ball she had to make a speech at. She'd never worn a dress, not that I'd seen anyway, and had made a panic purchase at Fraser's. It wasn't horrible, but it wasn't her, and she looked uncomfortable in it. I raced out and bought her a floaty trouser ensemble. She rocked it.

A few years ago, I signed her up for a dating site. She was mortified, but she went on a few dates, and while she didn't meet anyone special, she started taking better care of herself after that.

Mum didn't always know what was best for her. Sometimes I was the better judge.

I had to get there in time. It did matter! I needed to be with her went she left. Don't let it be too late.

The cars ahead of me were driving up the ramp onto the ferry.

I U-turned with a screech and headed south at seventy miles an hour.

The police booked me at Tarbet, and there was an accident just before Luss, which meant it was almost midnight when I arrived back at Dear Green Care Home. Don't let it be too late. Don't let it be too late.

*

No one was answering the door. I raced round to the back, rang Marcus's bell. No answer. Tried the door. Locked. Ran round to the front again, knocked, buzzed, banged on the office window. Finally, Harriet opened the door.

She looked shocked to see me; pale, even. Oh God, no! I barged past her, ignoring whatever she was saying to try and stop me.

I took a breath at Mum's door, knowing what I might find when I opened it.

She wasn't there.

I don't know how long I was on the floor, crying, before Rose came in.

'Catherine?'

'Rose, you should be asleep.'

'They tried to give me the drugs again, but I only pretended to swallow. Quick, get out of here before they catch you.' She put the hairgrip she'd used to escape from her room back in her blackcurrant hair.

'Before who catches me?'

'If I tell you a secret, do you promise not to tell?'

'Rose, let me help you to bed.'

She pointed to the back of the house. 'Shh!' She had that same look of terror she had the first day I met her, when Nurse Gabriella had popped a pill in her mouth and left her in bed. When Gabriella had gone, she'd opened her eyes and pressed her finger to her mouth: 'Shh!'

'Come, let's get you back to bed.'

Harriet had disappeared somewhere. It was so quiet tonight, everyone sound asleep. I wondered if the ambulance had taken her already.

As I tucked Rose in, I noticed she'd been clawing at the tag on her ankle. There were small cut marks in the rubber, deep gashes in her flesh.

'Your breathing's getting worse, Margie!'

'Rose, it's all right. I'm fine.'

She rubbed my hand. 'You're so cold, Margie. I'll light a fire. Sit still, warm yourself by the flames, I'll be back. Oh, I need matches. I'll be back in no time.'

'Okay, Rose.' She was too weak to get up. Her eyes were closing. 'Okay, I'll do that. It's okay, Rose.'

I noticed on her desk that she'd started drawing another picture, but had only managed to draw the door, with Room 7 written on it, and a camera in the corner of the room.

*

I could see the light was on in Room 7 from the crack under the door. I turned the handle, not expecting it to be locked.

I heard Harriet whispering to someone and I started to feel angry, desperate to see Mum's face, to hold her.

'Let me in!' I didn't care if I woke anyone up. 'Harriet, open the door NOW!'

More whispering. A man's voice this time.

When Harriet opened the door a few inches, I noticed her cheeks were heart-attack red. She was sweating. I pushed past her.

Marcus was in the room, standing between me and the bed. I pushed him aside and there she was.

They'd brushed her thick greying hair, which made it all boofy. She hated her hair boofy. She had foundation, mascara, and lipstick on. Mum didn't wear make-up. She was dressed in a silky silver nightie. This nightie wasn't hers! Her favourite jammie bottoms were pink polka dot, thin cotton. They had done everything wrong. How dare they?

A noise. I placed my cheek against her mouth. She was alive.

'Why did you move her?'

Marcus stood, spoke softly: 'Just . . . Catherine, I know it's hard, but you shouldn't be here. People regret not doing what their loved ones wanted, thinking only of themselves at a time like this. You don't get a second chance. It stays with you, the rest of your life.'

'I'm moving her back to her room. Get out of my way.'

He stood between me and Mum, arms up. 'I'm afraid

I must insist that you leave. In her advanced care planning—'

'If you don't get out of my way, I'll call the police.'

He thought for a moment, then stood aside. I pushed the brakes off the wheels of the trolley bed, and wheeled her out the door, down the hall, and back into her own room.

I called the cougar doctor, who hadn't come this afternoon to administer morphine, as I'd been told. She set it up now, assuring me Mum wouldn't have been in any pain, and that the staff had probably been waiting until she was. The doctor left to talk to Marcus and Harriet. I heard them in the office. They sounded like they were arguing. The doctor had probably lied to me about Mum's pain levels, so I wouldn't get upset. She should have been called earlier. Mum should have been on morphine for hours. I took off the incongruous silk nightie and put on her polka-dot jammie trousers and white sleeveless T-shirt. I wiped her face with a warm flannel. I put some product in her hair to flatten it. No make-up, just her lovely face. She had such perfect skin, my mum. Smooth as mine. I shut the blinds to keep out the lights. The doctor drove off. A few cars drove in. Then left again. I'd ask Marcus about that later, the liar. I put a sponge of water to her mouth. I stroked her arm. I kissed her cheek. I talked to her.

About my first memory of her. I was three, or four.

She had to go to work, and left me at Gran's house to bake fairy cakes. I cried. I didn't want her to go.

About my first boyfriend. I was fifteen. She didn't like him. She was right not to like him.

About my first job. I was twenty-three. She organised it for me. It was the hardest and the best experience of my life.

I talked and I talked and I cried and I cried and—

Maureen died at 4.55 a.m.

She had wanted to die in bed, in her room in Dear Green Care Home. She had wanted to die alone. No music, no priest.

She died in her room in Dear Green Care Home. No music, no priest. Her daughter Catherine was holding her hand.

Her final words: 'That's not music, is it?'

Her last breath: like a sigh.

She looked very tired.

There was no reflection in her eye.

There is no jpeg.

One Week Prior to Death

CHAPTER SEVENTEEN

Everyone at Dear Green was sorry for my loss. I am sorry
for your loss, said Marcus, said Gavin, said the cougar
doctor, said Harriet, said the ambulance driver. I am sad
for your misplacement, I am apologetic for your failure.
Nonsensical!

Rose didn't say that. She stood with me as my loss exited the drive. She helped me pack my loss's suitcase. She
kissed me after I cut her tag off with a Swiss army knife
and said: 'Bad things happen here, Catherine.'

I gave her my mum's mobile phone. 'Turn it on here.
Press 1 for me, 2 for the police.' I made Rose practise
ringing me a few times. 'The ringer's off but it'll vibrate
very quietly if I ring you, like this: *bzzz*. Have you got
somewhere to hide it?'

I watched as she lifted the bedside cabinet and tilted
it so it leant against the bed. Underneath the unit, she'd
taped half a dozen stuffed envelopes, a few fifty-pound
notes poking out of one, and over twenty packets of
matches. She took some tape from the art materials on
her desk, and taped the phone there too.

I forgot to ask Marcus about the cars that had come and gone last night. I went home to look for my loss in the clothes I'd rescued from Oxfam, in the three photo albums Mum had carefully compiled for me, in jobs just done, in the freezer. I wasn't hungry, but even if I had been, I couldn't have eaten the dead food, only slightly colder than she was now, probably. I couldn't throw it out either. Thoughtful, misguided Mum.

Curtains drawn, lights off, I put on her favourite windcheater, lay on the sofa, photo albums open and spread out on the coffee table, the teddy she gave me for my fifth birthday at my chest, and waited for tears to fill some space, some time, but they didn't come. I urged them: the photos on my phone in Rothesay would do it. Ten selfies taken on the ferry; me and Mum making funny faces, laughing. No, no relief, just a rumbling stomach as empty as the rest of me.

The phone rang twice but I didn't answer. Antonio with a kind 'Hey, Cath, I've heard. Call me.' And Paul: 'Are you there? Can I come over?'

What I needed now was to rummage through boxes for insurance documents, to pay bills that hadn't been paid, to tidy away the mess that illness makes, to organise a funeral. I rang the funeral director Mum had decided to use and he reassured me that everything had been done: music, eulogy, humanist minister booked; he'd invited everyone on the small invitation list, organised the catering at St Jude's after. 'All you need to do is turn up at ten on Monday.'

Misguided Mum! She'd taken away all the rituals that keep people going in the dark days that follow death. I didn't even have any family to fall out with. What I'd do to yell at a brother for trying to steal the inheritance, to punch at a sister for taking the ring I wanted, to make a regretful remark to a grief-stricken father: I wish it was you!

A father! Mum had left me the number of his parents. Where was it? In one of those envelopes. I dialled the number without thinking. 'Hello, this is Catherine Mann, can I please speak to Mr or Mrs Marks?'

'This is Mrs Marks speaking.'

I already hated the posh clipped voice of Mrs Marks, my grandmother. I decided to remain aloof, matter of fact, just passing on some information, that's all. 'I'm Maureen Mann's daughter. Your son was my biological father. I'm just ringing to let you know that Maureen died last night.'

Mrs Marks didn't speak for a moment. I waited for the tears and the speech – You poor sweet thing, all alone in the world. Come here, live here! You are all we have of our beloved son! Take our money! Be ours! Instead: 'I'm sorry for your loss, Catherine . . .'

I hung up. I kissed the sapphire ring on my finger: my gran's ring, my mum's, now mine.

And then I did what I always used to do to avoid real life. I went online.

I read articles and blog posts about the stages of grief. I scanned conversations on forums, where people talked about the loss of a parent. I Googled Mum. Maureen Mann had 49,000 search results on Google. *Managing Director opens new school in Zimbabwe. Maureen Mann on forced marriage. Maureen Mann, keynote speaker at Heywood Charity Ball.* Ms Mann says this about injustice and that about poverty and this about a new government policy and that about generosity. The most recent result was written in one the of the blogs related to her charity titled *RIP Maureen Mann*, which used words like saddened, passing, brave, battle, dedicated, tireless, inspirational, survived by her—

Stop!

Rose Price had 349,870 search results on Google, pages and pages of photos of her at fifty, fifty-six, sixty-three, sixty-five, all the way up to four years ago, when she did a reading at the Edinburgh Book Festival. So successful and pretty and happy and sharp-looking! I Googled myself. There were lots of Catherine Manns: a lawyer, an economist, and some young idiot on Twitter

whose posts were always about being drunk or hung-
over. (Me.)

I messaged Gina and Rebecca.

Mum died last night. I'm not up to seeing anyone at
the moment. No pressure, but the funeral's Monday
at ten. Clydebank Crematorium.

I Googled Jimmy – Jim Thornton. There were 7,050
search results for him. A few articles about some members of his old band trying to make a comeback. Two
about the lead singer who'd died of an overdose a year
since. He'd been done with Internet offences in 2003.
No details, except that when his neighbours found out
two years ago they firebombed his living room. After
that, he'd moved into a care home.

I checked Facebook. Gina and Rebecca had both seen
my message, neither had replied. Composing would take
time, probably.

I Googled Marcus Baird. Lo and behold, he had a
blog: *It's no Fun to Be Yellow – Marcus Baird on Writing*.

His posts were as dull as his book – 'Coping with
Writer's Block', 'The Genre Debate', 'Views on Perspec-
tive', and '*The Little Death* – read the first chapter for
free here'. No one commented on any of them, and no
wonder.

I Googled *The Little Death*. Someone had already

written a book called that, the dickwad. A bestseller, too. If it was me, I'd use the French expression. What was it again? *La petite mort*. Don't know why I Googled that or why I clicked on the first page of links, but I did.

Link ten produced a blank screen with just the title: 'La Petite Mort'. It had the same background colour and the same font as Marcus's blog. Under the title was a box: 'Enter Referral Code 1 here'.

My phoned beeped – a text from Paul, same as the voice message: *You okay? Can I come over?*

I'm okay. Getting some rest. You mind? Think I need alone time. See you Monday x

I scanned my texts. God, Natalie had left so many messages:

Can we meet up?

Sorry to be annoying, but can we meet up?

Is this the number for an alarm or something? It was in the logbook on the day a woman called Carmel Tate died, eighteen months ago: zKgy48r9fP2_9b

Call me.

Please, it's urgent. Call me.

I'm not a thief. Rose gave me those pictures but
three years later she forgot. So I gave them back.
Can you please call me?

Lots of missed calls after that.

I tried her number, but it went straight to voicemail. I
Googled her. The last entry for her was an article in the
Herald written six months ago.

Social Worker Found Not Guilty of Theft.

Natalie Holland, accused of stealing a large collec-
tion of original drawings from famous writer Rose
Price, was found not guilty in Glasgow Sheriff Court
today. Ms Price, now suffering from dementia, had
accused her social worker of theft, but later reneged
on the allegation. 'I gave them to her,' Ms Price said
later in interviews. 'She did not steal them. I was
confused when I said that.' While Ms Price's grandson and her lawyers argued that Ms Price's
retraction was unreliable, Sheriff Miller argued that
the initial accusation was similarly unreliable, and
found Ms Holland not guilty.

She wasn't a thief, then. Wasn't crazy. I went back to her
first text and typed the code into the website I'd found,
not expecting for a moment that it'd work.

And it didn't.

I badly needed a funeral to organise.

I checked Facebook. Gina had come back:

I'm so sad for you, honey! Please can I come over
and see you?

That was better than expected.

Rebecca, however, had not replied.

I opened a Word document and stared for so long that I synchronised my blinks with the cursor. I could just imagine the eulogy Mum had prepared. A factual thank-you speech, like the ones she gave for her charity events. She was an excellent public speaker. I didn't want an excellent speech. I wanted one that'd make the people she'd invited weep.

Mu mum. I retyped, realising I'd made a mistake: *My Mum*, no, *My mum*. Nothing else came. All the ideas in my head were facts and thank yous. Perhaps Mum's eulogy was the only kind you could really do at a funeral.

God, my typing was atrocious.

I opened the website again, retyped the password very carefully. Maybe I'd made a mistake.

zKgy48r9fP2_9b, then repeated it, as requested.

This time, another page opened, grey background. The only words: This site requires special software, download here for £34.99.

I needed to cry.

I closed it down, cried, and fell asleep.

*

Would you rather grief or anger? Anger. Would you grief or a broken nose? A broken nose. Grief or greed? Greed. In the days that followed Mum's death, I chose obsession. Over a password. This seemed far better than a freezer filled with dead food and a heart filled with nothing.

I'd paid £34.99 for the software at 4 a.m. Friday morning, now installed on my MacBook, and another page had opened asking me for Referral Code 2. I had no real reason to be obsessed. Once I started, it just took me over. Like making the decision to stay on hold to British Gas. You simply cannot back down.

In desperation, I tried zKgy48r9fP2_9b again. Incorrect. Marcus had to be behind the website. The font, the title, the colour of the background. What would he choose as a code? I focused exclusively on him. Baird, Mbarid, mbaird, marcusb and every permutation of his name possible, writing down each and crossing it off if it didn't work. This took all of Friday morning.

I don't recall much about Paul's visit on Friday afternoon. Before letting him in, I must have hidden the dozens of pieces of printing paper covered in possible passwords. Soup was involved, and I assume he must have put a blanket over me, as I woke late that night to find it there; a glass of water, two Valium and a note on the coffee table: 'You might want one of these at night, to calm you down. Please call me when you wake.'

I spent Friday night typing in words relating to Dear Green. You'd be surprised how many there were, especially if you use capitals and lower case and numbers. Seven hours and I believed I'd exhausted that idea.

Saturday and Sunday I moved on to what I knew about his book, *The Little Death*. I read the chapter he'd put online, using character and place names, playing around with the English title and the French translation.

People knocked on my door a few times. I think, anyway. I heard the rustle of paper being posted through the door. Notes from Paul, Antonio, probably. Possibly Gina and Rebecca. I didn't bother to look, too busy.

When I woke Monday morning, I realised the living room was covered in pieces of paper which were covered in incorrect access codes. What on earth? Avoidance they'd call it, I suppose, or madness. I gathered the sheets of paper, tossed them in a bin bag, and had a shower. Looking through my wardrobe later, I noticed a sweet black dress on a hanger, tag still on. Mum had even bought my funeral outfit.

*

A fat woman in a trouser suit worked through Mum's agenda:

1. *Welcome.*
2. *Eulogy.*
3. *Song. The one she used to sing to me, 'Feelin' Good' by Nina Simone, played as the coffin disappeared behind the cheap curtain.*
4. *Cocktails, sandwiches, cakes (at St Jude's).*

All forty-three people there knew Mum well, and loved her. She chose her mourners wisely. Paul and Antonio didn't budge from my side as colleagues and friends and two aunts and three uncles and five cousins and Rebecca and Gina expressed their sorrow for my loss, adding a more meaningful one-liner to the usual blurb – She was the kindest boss I ever had. She never stopped talking about how proud she was of you. She didn't realise how beautiful she was. She was just so honest, the least phony person I've ever known. She never forgot a birthday. She was cool. Yeah, there was not an ounce of phony in her.

'Thank you,' I said, 'thank you so much.'

I felt heavy, that's the only word I can think of. Heavy. Like the earth should crack underneath from the weight of my feet. Like my legs couldn't hold my torso up, my neck couldn't hold my head up. I wanted that earth to give way, so I could sink down into it. I remember the video screen at the foyer of the crematorium. Maureen Mann, it said. *That's my mum's name*, I thought. A lot of people wept during the service. But my tears were as heavy as the rest of me and stayed behind my eyes. I remember someone asking me if I wanted to see her before we went into the service and me saying, 'No.' I know I'd seen her as a body already, but only just after she died, and while she did look different, her expression set as a dead one, I hadn't adjusted enough to the new state of things to be appalled by it, for her to be a stranger. I didn't want to see her now. I wanted to forget ill Mum, dead Mum; to remember her well and alive. I sat at the front, knowing everyone behind was looking at me, thinking, *Poor Catherine, all alone,* and I didn't cry and I didn't turn around to smile and make them feel better about me.

At St Jude's I sat between Paul and Antonio and picked at a fairy cake, accepting hugs and sorries as they came, leaving as soon as it seemed appropriate. Paul dropped me off, begged to come in. 'Thanks, Paul. But I want to be alone.' He hugged me, said he'd check on me later.

And that was the funeral: efficient, gentle, appropriate, sad, loving.

*

Back at home, alone, I took off the sweet black dress Mum had bought for me and lay on my bed. What was I supposed to do now?

I got up, grabbed a suitcase from the hall cupboard, and began packing for Costa Rica. I was loaded now. I could change the flight and leave immediately. Perfect. I packed my bikinis, my summer dresses, summer shoes, sunglasses, bright, happy things, then looked in the mirror . . . Why had I wanted to go to Costa Rica? To dance on beaches and drink in bars. I couldn't imagine wanting to dance again, or drink in bars with strange men who I'd seduce then chuck three weeks later. I shoved the packed suitcase back in the hall cupboard.

I needed Mum to tell me what to do next. I needed a meeting, with an agenda. I looked through all the envelopes she'd left – mortgage, car, funeral . . . none labelled 'What you should do now.'

If she had, what would she have written? I thought about the way she described me to others – Catherine is very kind. She has always looked after me. She has always wanted to do good. She doesn't care about money or status.

She'd tell me to do a postgrad in social work, and she'd be right. She was always right. Her mourners were spot on. She was the cleverest, and the least phony person I've ever known. Not an ounce of phony in her.

I took a piece of paper and began the first list I had

ever written for myself. Before I knew it, the page was
filled with my hopes and dreams, and I was filled with
optimism that I would do five-fifths of them.

1. Be with Paul.
2. Get reference from Marcus.
3. Apply for postgrad in social work.
4. Read the Guardian online each morning.
5. Watch the Channel Four News.
6. Do an evening class in Spanish.
*7. Spend less time with Gina and Co/expand social
circle.*
8. Read a book a week.
9. Join the gym. Get fit.
10. Be with Paul.
11. Make Mum proud. Be like her. Don't be phony.

Phony . . . I hadn't used this word ever. Now, it seemed
to be coming up all the time. Phony. *Catcher in the Rye.*

I opened my laptop, the Enter Your Password box
daring me with its flicker.

I typed catcherintherye.

No, I would not become obsessed again. I would get
on with my life, my list. Do something that made sense,
something that mattered. I would – after one more try:

catcherrye

Just one more.

ryecatcher

LA PETITE MORT

Hello, Guest!

Welcome to La Petite Mort's forum. Here, you can
ask questions and share your experience with
others. Join the conversation!

New user? Register <u>here.</u>

Registering wasn't hard. Three questions altogether:
Age, Sex, Location. I became a fifty-nine-year-old male
from Aberdeenshire called tex59. After registering and
choosing my own password, I turned my computer off,
annoyed at myself for ignoring a very impressive and
sensible list, one I now knew I wanted to work my way
through. Okay, so Marcus had some super secure web-
sitey type thing, and was a weirdo who lied about cars
coming and going in the middle of the night, but what
did I care? Mum had done her business with Dear Green
and it had worked out almost as she planned. We'd had
quiet time together there. I'd grown up. I'd learned how
to care for her. She'd felt safe with me by her side. Job
done. So walk away, Catherine. Walk away from meaningless online activities that encourage you to take gap
years from living. Walk away, no need to read on . . .

Subject: I lost my mom by grievingme9

grievingme9: On the 2nd of February 2012, Dad called to say Mum was very poorly and I should get to the hospital. She was 63 and fit as a fiddle. Turns out she'd had a heart attack. When I arrived at accident and emergency, she'd already had another one. Dad and I watched as they tried to resuscitate her for over fifteen minutes. All that thumping on her chest, it felt abusive, you know? I'll never forget how she looked after. Never.

elvishasleft: Think you're on the wrong forum, love.

caulfield: No, we can talk about anything here. Sorry about your mum, grievingme9. Welcome to the forum. I know how it feels. My girlfriend died when I was eighteen. I'll never forget the feel of her skin when I kissed her goodbye.

caulfield: And who's this tex59? Can see you're lurking. Who are you?

elvishasleft: You undercover, tex59? You wanting to catch some pervs? Nothing here, mate, nothing here – just folk wanting to talk about their losses.

tex59: Not undercover. I'm just someone who wants to talk too.

elvishasleft: Like you wouldn't say that! Hey, I'm not undercover!!

tex59: Not sure how I can prove it. Want me to scan my passport?

elvishasleft: Yeah.

caulfield: No need, but want more info, tex59. Who gave you the codes?

tex59: A like-minded friend who trusted me. Isn't that how this works? Word of mouth?

I was taking a gamble, guessing this was how people found the site.

caulfield: We prefer to think of it as referrals from the like-minded, but fair enough. What's your mind like?

tex59: I'm someone who'd like to know what your girlfriend's skin felt like.

caulfield: Her skin felt like raw chicken. Go feel some.

tex59: Going . . . Ah, see what you mean.

I didn't, obviously. I didn't even have raw chicken, only frozen.

grievingme9: I think we're gonna have a lotta fun here.

tex59: Is this all there is?

caulfield: What you mean?

tex59: Is this just for talking?

grievingme9: Yeah, there more or what?

elvishasleft: Maybe.

caulfield: Maybe not.

tex59: Tell.

caulfield: Newbies have to post a pic before we tell.

tex59: What like?

caulfield: Something proves we're like-minded.

tex59: Where to?

caulfield: Attach it to this thread. Do not send anything by email or post a link. And you can't just grab something online. You must have something saying La petite mort, your username and the date in the shot.

tex59: This like an initiation?

caulfield: Aye. And don't worry, I'll delete the pic immediately after and put it somewhere even safer.

grievingme9: Onto it.

tex59: Back soon . . .

*

Marcus was obviously caulfield. I had no idea who the
others were. I also had no idea what kind of fucked-up
picture they expected me to send, and if I could do it.
But I had to know what else was on that site. I walked
around the house looking for ideas. Would frozen chick-
en interest them? What if I lay down on my bed and
looked dead? I could drive to a country road and set myself up to look like roadkill. Hmm . . . chicken too tame,
the others too public.

The phone rang and I listened to Paul's message. 'Hey
you, I don't think you should be alone. I'm bringing you
food at eight. You have no choice in the matter. See you
then.'

Paul! His dad's abattoir! I packed a few things and
drove out of the city towards Fintry. It was ten to five
when I stopped fifty metres from the driveway. The shed
was in a beautiful setting, about half a mile from Paul's
family home. I watched the last of the workers leave, his
dad locking the large doors, then got out of the car with
my bag of props and scoured the building to find a way
in. All the doors had been locked, but there was a small

243

window at the back which was open. A few minutes later I was hanging upside down, knees curled over a metal pole attached to the ceiling. I only had pants and a sleeveless T-shirt on. The T-shirt fell just below my bra, so you could see tex59, La Petite Mort and the date written in red lip liner on one side of my stomach. My head was covered in a hessian bag, tied with a string. Beside me, hooves on hooks, was a dead pig, its stomach slit open, insides spilling. I let my head fall limp and took several selfies, hoping one of them would turn out okay.

*

I hesitated for ages before posting the picture. I looked as dead as the pig, and it felt so wildly wrong. Eventually I did, though, then sat on the sofa and stared at the screen, hoping a response would arrive before Paul did.

CHAPTER EIGHTEEN

AGE 82

Holy shit, she understood, and it had made her sick on the carpet. Did it happen again last night? Oh dear oh dear, what had they done to her friend? She had to call Chris. No! Not Chris. The police. No! They never believed a thing she said, and no wonder. Catherine! She had her phone number somewhere. Catherine had given it to her before she left. Where was it? In the small silver book in her desk? No, that small book was all wrong. It had numbers in it, but not the right kind. Had she tapped it into her phone. No, her phone was long gone, taken.

She looked through all the books on the shelves: pictures and words, no numbers. She emptied her drawers – clothes, no numbers. She counted out loud in case she'd read or heard the number and it came back to her. 1-2-3, but the one after that didn't even come to her. 1. Was her number 1? Of course not! She looked in the bathroom, under the bed. She tilted the bedside cabinet so it leant against the bed. Money and boxes of matches were taped to the bottom, and something else – what was that? – but no number. She looked under the mattress, under the pillows. There was no number and of course there was no number under the pillows! And why was she looking for numbers anyway? Remember, remember Rose. Sick on the floor. Something had made her vomit. She felt dizzy, sat at her desk, took some slow breaths. Before vomiting she'd written something, a red-biro scrawl.

ROSE – BELIEVE YOURSELF. It is sick and dangerous here. You're not writing this down because of the maze. Ring Catherine! Tell her to get the police. They might believe her. They never believe you and they are wrong.

Catherine! But where did she live? Was it in Glasgow? Was what in Glasgow?

Catherine! She had no time to dither in this dungeon. She had to hurry.

There was no one around. The only noises were coming from Nancy's room. Rose picked her lock open, walked across the hall, and peeked in – Gavin was sitting in the armchair, pillow on lap, watching the television. All clear. Note in hand, she raced to the front door and across the field.

AGE 10

It was difficult to light a fire in the rain. The twigs were all damp, every single one. These northern twigs would probably always be wet. She scrunched the sheet of paper in her hand into a loose ball, covered it with the driest twigs she'd managed to find, carefully placed them in a teepee shape on top, and – bum! – she had no matches. She'd have to go back to the farmhouse and get matches. She ran as fast as she could, but she must have made a wrong turn, because the farmhouse wasn't where it should be. Where was she? Oh God, where had she left Margie? By the tree. Where was the tree? By the river, by the bend in the river. What bend? Where was the river? There was no river, just fields to the left, fields to the right, fields everywhere. No river, no trees. Oh God, Margie, poor Margie, where had she left her? She was lost! She stamped her feet, stamped and stamped. 'You're a selfish girl, Rose Price! A selfish, selfish girl!' She collapsed to the ground, and didn't mind that the earth scratched at her face. She deserved it.

CHAPTER NINETEEN

I'd heard nothing an hour later. The forum had gone quiet except for that grievingme9 person yapping on about his or her mother's death in a very uncomfortable way. I closed my eyes, exhausted, and slept until my mobile rang.

'Catherine?'

'Yeah . . .'

'It's Rose's grandson, Chris. I hope you don't mind, I got your number from Marcus. I'm calling because Rose ran away a while ago and I wondered if she'd gone to yours. Her tag was found under her bed. She must have cut it off.'

'No, she's not here. I don't think she knows where I live. Have you called the police?'

'Of course. They'll check the area but they're busy so I don't know how quickly they'll get onto it. I'm on my way back from Aberdeen and can't go out myself – just wanted to check with you.'

'What about her old house, or Natalie's?'

A long pause before: 'Of course.'

'I can go see.'

'No, no. Leave it, it's fine. I'm sure she'll be okay. Thanks.'

'Are you sure?'

He'd already hung up.

*

I rang Natalie straight away – left a message on her voicemail. I jumped in the car and drove to Natalie's house. Cutting the tag had seemed the right thing to do at the time, but now . . . oh God, I hoped Rose hadn't tried to get across the river again.

I tried Natalie's back door when she didn't answer the front. No luck. A prying neighbour poked her head over the hedge to scold me. 'Should you be in there?'

'Just wondering where Natalie is.'

'Who are you?'

'Sorry – I'm Catherine Mann. A friend of hers, a mutual friend of Rose Price. Is Natalie around?'

'No, actually, Brian's beside himself with worry because she didn't come home last night. He dropped the boys with me so he could go look for her.'

There was a lot of noise coming from the neighbour's garden. Natalie's boys were kicking a football around, laughing.

'Did he call the police?'

'Not yet. She'd started doing some agency work. He

thinks she might have just got caught up in an emergency.'

Before I drove home I tried Natalie's number again. Voicemail. Tried Chris's, switched off. Tried Dear Green. No answer.

As I drove to Dear Green, I wondered if someone there was grievingme9 and elvishasleft. I supposed sickos gravitated to each other, and what better place than a house full of dying people.

Harriet was flustered. 'You can't just barge in here now!' But I already had. Rose's room was empty, and she'd not drawn a new page since I left, or at least I couldn't find one. If she had, they'd probably thrown it out like all the others.

Room 7 was locked, as ever. There were well over fifty used paper cups in the bin by the water cooler. Last night was a busy night, by the looks.

Harriet was following me around. 'The police are looking for her. Catherine, you really can't come in here like this.'

'Did someone die last night?'

'No. Catherine, and I know this is a hard time for you, but I'm going to have to ask you to leave now.'

I tossed the cup back in the bin with the others. 'Okay, I'm off.' As I passed Room 3, Jimmy hollered.

'Hey, lovely!'

Harriet was at my heels. 'Is it all right if I say hi to Jim?'

'Five minutes.' She shrugged, and headed to the kitchen.

Jimmy was lying in bed in his pyjamas. I closed his door and kept my distance. 'Did someone die last night?'

'No. I'm still here!'

'Have you seen Rose?'

'No. Hey, don't s'pose you got any more of that grass? It was nice! A giggly one. What was it, Hawaiian Snow? It was so good to giggle!'

He wasn't comfortable with the pause, maybe knew what was coming. 'I know about you, Jimmy.'

'Ah, you know.' I expected him to be mortified, embarrassed, remorseful, or at least full of excuses. Instead: 'I did my time, Catherine.'

He held my stare. I think I felt more threatened by his than he did by mine. I left.

When I turned my head to avoid seeing Mum's room I spotted Gavin reading to Nancy in their room. He looked like a very sweet old man. The nausea was rising. I raced out to the driveway, lowered my head to bring the blood back, and took several long slow breaths. Surrounding my feet were fresh tyre tracks, everywhere, loads of them.

I peeked into the window of Room 7 from the back of the house. I hadn't noticed this when I found Mum lying in there, but the glass had been fixed since Rose smashed it, jail-like metal bars had been bolted to the outside, and new curtains had been installed. I couldn't see inside at all.

Marcus didn't answer his door, but it was open, so I let myself in. The place was a mess. Bottles and overflowing ashtrays everywhere. He was fully clothed, asleep on the sofa in the drawing room, mouth half open. He'd had a party last night. I didn't try to wake him. He revolted me. This place scared me. I had to get away.

I ran to the tree by the river, but Rose wasn't there. She had been recently, by the looks. A perfectly formed teepee-style fire had been set, ready for the matches she probably went hunting for afterwards. She must have wandered off from here, and got lost.

I dialled Mum's old mobile, hoping Rose had remembered where she hid it, and how to use it. It rang out. I decided I should go home, in case she found out where I lived, and headed there.

*

When I got home, I rang Natalie and Chris again. Still no answer from Natalie, and no sign of Rose, Chris said. I was about to phone the police when a message popped up on the forum:

caulfield: Ah, so you're one of those. We have quite a few like you.

tex59: Really! I'd love to see what they're into. What can you show me?

caulfield: There are rules.

tex59: That's fine.

caulfield: Delete the pic you just sent and this conversation. I'll remove it from the server. Click on Explore at the bottom of the site. Username: itscutetobedead. Password: 3hguz9c7dC.

tex59: Great, thanks.

caulfield: Now delete, delete, delete.

tex59: Pinky promise.

*

I braced myself, fully expecting to be shocked and disgusted by pictures like mine – of raw meat, dead animals, perhaps nakedness, I couldn't imagine what else, but when I clicked Explore I journeyed far deeper than shock and disgust. Once there, it seemed impossible to return to the surface, where people worked as accountants and bus drivers, fell in and out of love, had mis-

sionary sex with their partners two to three times per
week, grieved for their loved ones by crying and organising funerals and falling out over money and throwing
out dead flowers. 'There's something for everyone online,' Chris had said once.

<u>At La Petite Mort we believe the following</u>:

Birth, sex and death are the most intense experien-
ces.

Intensity is pleasurable.

In Shakespeare's time, orgasms were referred to as
'little deaths'. This is because sexual climax and
death are similar. The moment of death arouses
sexual feelings.

Death is helpless transcendence.

Helplessness is sexy.

Someone with power over life and death is power-
fully attractive.

If you are involved in, or witness to a death, you feel
sexy.

You are God.

*

<u>At La Petite Mort, we share our first experiences</u>:

friskycorpse: My dad was a butcher. He took me to the slaughter house when I was five. I can remember when I first played dead there, lying on the slab beside a sheep. I took my best friend once and he played dead with me. He wasn't good at it, wriggled and got bored. It was my favourite game. Still is.

bestdirector: My aunty was a film buff. She took me to the movies once a week, started sneaking me into the 18s when I was fifteen. The first death scene I remember watching was *Wild at Heart*. Anyone seen this? Oh wow, when that girl in the car crash dies in front of them! Picks at her brain! After that, I used to buy DVDs with my fave scenes in, replay and replay. I remember the first time I masturbated to one. *The Wicker Man.* (Ha, I know! I was easily aroused as a teen!) Mum and Dad were at tennis so I locked the door and took my time. So powerful! I never looked back. How good is it to talk to people who don't think this is abnormal! I love this site. Thanks La Petite Mort. xxxx

coolzombie: LOL friskycorpse! My fave game was morgue. (Lucky there was one in our basement, eh!! Dad's a funeral director.) Best game ever. Couldn't get my mates into it but. You're so right, this site is amazeballs. Makes me feel okay about myself, you know, like I'm not the only one.

burkenhare: You're really not the only one frisky-corpse! Why do people find death so ugly? It's beautiful. Is there anything more beautiful?

And hello Marcus:

caulfield: My first time was when I was fifteen. She had translucent Irish skin. I was in love with that skin. I've never said this to anyone, but I climaxed when she died without even touching myself. I still remember the outline of her nipples. After that, I began to see it everywhere, probably because of what my parents did, where I lived and still live. I won't give too much away here, but death was all around. I saw it, and began noting details. I was fascinated in the difference between how people hope to die and how they actually die. I started taking pics. It's fascinating, isn't it? I wondered if you could see the hope extinguished as it happens, replaced by disappointment or anger, or doused by pain. Or perhaps hope is the wrong word — not many hope to die. I was also interested in the afterlife at the time — could they see it as they left their bodies? Was another world there, at the end of their beds?

I'm not interested in that so much now – an adolescent fear had made me obsess about heaven and hell I think. Now it's the beauty of it, the power of it, that gets me. Ah, it's so good to talk. And to write about it! Btw, top tip – pretend you're writing a crime novel, then you can write whatever turns you on, and research all you like, and you have an excuse if anyone catches you at it! It's a safety net for me. I remember how good it felt when I posted a pic here for the first time. I didn't leave my bedroom till a reply came, which it did, two days later, and that's how I met elvishasleft, hey Elvis!

elvishasleft: Sure thing roomie!

grievingme9: Its looked down on like all taboos I guess. Biggest taboo of em all – so how could you not want to go there! Your a voyeur, invading the most private moment. Your god like.

deathrattle: It's not like they don't want it! You have brain surges at the moment of death, men get boners. It's a fact that many men who have been hanged have ejaculated the moment their necks snap. I know, I've seen it happen (not w hanging like!) My grandad had a stonker right before he went. And he was old as fuck, probs hadn't managed one of

them for years. It's sexy! Not like we're doing anything wrong.

devotedhusband: My wife and I had the shared
interest. Ah, I miss her. When we were courting –
that's a long time ago! – she asked me what I fantas-
ised about. I hadn't expected her to share my
interest before then, but I wonder if she had always
known, from the moment she laid eyes on me. Perhaps there is something in our eyes that beckons
kindred spirits. I was too scared to say at the time.
We were walking home from the movies. Then she
came out with it! Before we'd even kissed! Her
fantasy was to be dug from the grave and taken!
She's still here, but has dementia, can't speak,
doesn't even have facial expressions. Before it got
bad I promised her, promised again and again (she
made me!) that I would do this for her one day. And
I will. I don't know how I'll manage it (maybe you
could help me friskycorpse? Is your dad still in the
funeral business?) It's all I live for now. I still make
love to her all the time. I can't see the pleasure on
her face, but I KNOW it's there. I know I'm making
her proud.

That's a lovely story Gavin. How lucky, his catatonic
wife.

friskycorpse: I can do better than that devotedhusband. It's Dad and Son Funeral Directors! Let me
know when you need me. Happy to help a kindred
spirit.

elvishasleft: I was on my third UK tour with the band.
One night after a gig, one of the backup singers OD'd
on heroin. I don't think I could have saved her if I tried
but I know I couldn't stop doing what I was doing,
standing over her, watching, filming. I was off my head
too! Seemed magical, all of it, had to get it on tape.
That vid's still available, if you want a peek (go to
Movies then elvishasleft873). I watch it at least once a
week. Check how she looks into the camera, right into
it, at the very last second. As if the afterlife existed in
the lens and was calling her. Got hooked on filming
after that. Check out Movies 854-1058. All mine!
Huge variety. Can't say how this site changed my life.

Well, hey there, Jimmy.

*

Deeper, deeper, I went, all the way to the Photo Gallery.
I clicked into a world of dead people – babies, toddlers,
children, young adults, adults, middle-aged, the elderly.
I clicked and saw the naked dead, the mutilated dead,

the peaceful dead, the roadkill dead. I clicked and saw the living touching the dead, lying with the dead, having sex with the dead.

I threw up.

I rang Chris. He was out looking for Rose, sounded stressed. 'I've stumbled on something here, Chris. I'm going to call the police. Marcus, Jimmy, Gavin, they're all involved in a website called La Petite Mort.'

'What? How did you find that? Holy shit. Let me park. Stay on . . . Okay, I'm in a lay-by. Are you okay?'

'No! Chris, there's a video section and I can't bring myself to look at it.'

'Don't. Don't look at it. You could be charged! I'll call the police straight away. I know the ones who deal with this stuff. I'll call now. La Petite Mort?'

'Yeah.' I was crying. 'It's . . . it's beyond awful.'

'I'll call them now, get them to come straight over. You sure you're okay?'

'No, but . . . I will be. I'll wait here for the police. Tell them to come quickly!'

'Yeah, wait there. What's your address?'

'Dowanhill, 13 Dowanside Road.'

'Don't look at that shit, eh? Don't talk to anyone till the police come. Turn off your phones, lock the door.'

'Okay.'

'And don't let anyone in except the police.'

'Okay.'

*

I locked the front and back doors, turned off my mobile phone, and pulled out the landline socket. I was about to shut down the computer when I noticed the link to the <u>Movie</u> page at the top. Clicking the down arrow, I read through the different sub-pages, which included elvishasleft and about twenty other names which were probably linked to the amateur films sent by members of this community. I was repulsed by the idea of viewing any of the films, but when I noticed that one of the pages was labelled <u>Events</u>, I couldn't help myself.

<u>EVENTS</u>

This, written just before my mother died:

> Wednesday Special: 49-year-old female, attractive, has hair – salt and pepper. Movie scheduled for 12.30 a.m., give or take. Twelve Viewing tickets available at £200 per head. Cash. At door. Message to secure place, and for directions and further details. No phones and no cameras please.

And this, from last Thursday, just after my mother died.

> Apologies for last-minute cancellation of the Special

last night. It was beyond our control, I'm afraid. In the meantime, have you seen our most recent videos?

More events coming soon.

There were dozens of complaints under this post. People had driven for hours. People wanted a refund for petrol money. People were livid. People were losing faith in the service. People wanted to get in free next time.

And this, from yesterday:

Unscheduled Special tonight! We have a Sunday offering! Apologies for the short notice, but as you know we can't always plan these things. This will be worth your while! 45-year-old female, healthy, classy, slim but not emaciated, athletic, has hair, dark. £350 per head. Cash. At door. Message to secure a place, and for directions and further details. No phones and no cameras please.

The most recent post was entered this morning.

Record number of hits! Last night's Unscheduled Special an unprecedented triumph. Over 1,000 hits, growing by the minute. Click here and you'll see why! It also sparked a bidding war amongst 45 potential viewers. After they saw a pic of the star, they were willing to pay treble our initial price. Again, click <u>here</u> to see why. Congratulations La Petite Mort! 5*!!

Before I could stop myself, I had clicked <u>here</u>, to see why.

Before it started, I knew enough already. I knew that by defying my mum's wishes and turning round at the ferry ramp, I had saved her. I had saved her death. I realised Rose had meant to say this when she made her way to the police that day. She wanted to 'save deaths'. I knew that Rose had been right about everything all along: that people were not safe in Dear Green, that Wednesday's children were full of woe, this was not how they wanted things to go. I knew people watched live on the Internet, that some paid to go and watch in the room, that as they watched they 'died a little death'. I knew Marcus was beyond creepy. I knew Jimmy was a registered sex offender. I knew Gavin raped his vegetative wife. I didn't need to know any more. Surely there could be no more to know.

*

Sunday Special!

A blank screen: 1,087 views; 57 comments.

Awesome!

Cute before, adorable after!

You're spoiling us!

I cannot stop watching this.

I am never a going to stop watching this!

A moment later, the black of the screen was replaced by
a brightly lit Room 7. Crammed with watchers, at least
a dozen. More, I think. The camera showed only their
legs and feet. Mostly male shoes, three female, as far as
I could tell. All sorts of shoes too: trainers, sandals, polished brogues.

I don't know what I expected to see on the bed, but
when the camera finally settled there, I screamed. I
needed a paper bag to breathe into. I had to stop myself
from fainting. Natalie, on the bed. Poor Natalie.

What had Natalie said on the phone when I was driving north? It had been a bad line – half sentences. I'm
going to break . . . the next day or so, if he goes out. So
perhaps she broke into Marcus's flat and was caught in
the act.

Unscheduled Sunday Special! She was awake, but
very drowsy. Tears were running down her face. She
could only manage a faint 'My boys! My beautiful boys!'
Her meagre pleas caused noises from the watchers I did

not want to hear. Zips unzipping. Ah-ah-ahing. All the while, the hits at the bottom of the screen increasing. I slammed the laptop lid shut. And thank God, the doorbell rang. The police were here.

*

I had the chain on, and opened the door an inch to see who it was first. Not the police, but Chris. 'Chris! Oh come in, quick!' I unhooked the chain, opened the door. He shut it behind him, looking as sick and worried as I felt.

'You speak to anyone?'

'No. Holy shit, Chris, this is so awful. They killed Natalie.'

He followed me into the living room. 'You don't follow instructions.'

I'd reached the laptop, was about to show him what I'd found. 'What?'

'What did I tell you on the phone before?'

'Not to talk to anyone. I didn't.'

'That's right, good. But what else did I say?'

'Um . . .' He was walking towards me, too close. He had one hand behind his back, something in it. 'Um, you said not to . . .'

'I said don't look at that shit, and don't let anyone in. Except the police.'

265

Death

CHAPTER TWENTY

AGE 82

The Queen, red lips. The Queen, red lips. The Queen. Red lips.

Rose kept saying it, over and over, as she walked across yet another field, hoping she was walking in the right direction. She was drenched. She didn't know why. But she knew she had to get back to Dear Green.

The Queen, red lips.

The Queen, red lips.

Why was she saying that? Ah, that garage looked familiar. Was it the one near Dear Green? It looked like every other garage. Oh, but were there mirrors? There should be mirrors on sticks in the distance, at the end of the driveway. No, no mirrors. This wasn't the one where Chris sometimes bought her Doritos if she asked him nicely. Chris sometimes said: 'Sure, Gran, but you have to promise to chew them before swallowing. They're sharp, those things. Remember that time you didn't chew one properly? You nearly choked, didn't you?' He looked after her, that grandson of hers. He protected her, kept her safe. That bossy Chris boy. Chris, with beautiful chiselled features inherited from Vernon, with the pretty lips of a child inherited from no one, all his. Pretty lips. So red.

The Queen. Chris.

*

She was so cold. Why was she wet?

'Are you okay?' Someone had spotted her by the fuel pumps. 'You're all wet. What's your name?'

'I'm fine. I'm just on my way home.'

The man had two children in the car. Rose would use him in a book one day – that torn look on his face. He had two kids in the car. One was a toddler, crying. And there was a wet old lady wandering by parked trucks. Kids? Wet old lady? Kids? Wet old lady?

'Is home close?'

'I'm sure it is!' Rose kept walking, on the pavement now, passing a betting shop, a pound store, a bakery.

Three teenage boys laughed at her as she walked by. She'd write about them one day too. Kill them, maybe. Ha!

Red lips, red lips. Not good. Not good. Very bad, in fact. She'd wondered, since Chris took her to the exit to the maze. Greeted the owner like an old friend, un-packed her things, visited more often than all the other visitors joined together, and much more than he did when she was in the West End.

There were many good things about Chris. He had fabulous taste. He listened. He was kind. And very good looking. She hadn't had major concerns about him before Dear Green. Most nine-year-old boys would find a dead pigeon intriguing, wouldn't they? Perhaps not. But after she moved to Dear Green, Rose started to wonder about him. He spent a lot of time with the slimy owner, and lot of time in Jimmy's room.

And then he visited late one night, held her down while Harriet shoved two pills in her mouth. She pretended to fall asleep, listened as Chris tapped on his computer for a while, as Marcus opened the door to say: 'Quick, they're arriving. Hair and make-up!' and as Chris said, 'Right you are.'

Chris slapped her cheek to check she was unconscious, and left the room, shutting the door behind him. Then she spat out the pills. Another car was parking in the driveway. Why so many, at two in the morning? She wished Nurse Gabriella was on duty, but she'd left hours earlier. A dour-faced bitch, that nurse, but she had a good heart. Rose was too scared to leave her room. She could hear the back door opening, closing; a room at the back of the house opening, closing; she could see people walking from their cars around the side of the house. She knocked at the wall – a secret code between her and

Beatrice. Bang. Bang, bang-bang-bang-bang. Bea always knocked back, saying, 'I'm here, Rose, and I'm okay.' But she didn't this time. And then she saw Chris's laptop, still open on the desk by the window. It took her a while to understand what she was seeing – Bea, on a trolley bed. Chris was leaning over her face, touching up her lips until they were almost as red as his. Marcus and Jimmy were watching from the other side. Gavin wheeled Nancy in, taking their place around the bed.

Chris was coming. She jumped back in bed and pretended to sleep as he took his laptop. She pounced back out of bed, opened her door an inch and watched as he turned right at the end of the hall. A door closed. He'd gone into Room 7. *That's where Bea is*, Rose thought. *And they're filming her*. She should do something. She should ring someone, but where was her phone? She could use the one in the office. Use what one in what office?

Bzzz. Bzzz.

She checked the clock. 3.15 a.m. She must have been lost in the maze again for over an hour.

Bzzz. Harriet had picked up the intercom phone in the office adjacent. 'Yes sir,' she'd said, 'I'll get the kettle on.' She'd heard Harriet preparing food and drink in the dining room, then a crowd walking down the hall, entering the dining room, closing the door. She should check on Bea! Rose tiptoed down the empty hallway and turned the handle of Room 7. She didn't go in, just looked from a crack in the door. Bea! Salvia frothed noisily from her slack mouth. There was a camera on a tripod in the corner of the room. These people were watching Bea die. These people were filming her. She should get the police!

Rose closed her bedroom door just as the crowd in the dining room began pouring out again, and heading back to Bea. So intermission had only been ten minutes. Intermission?

And then some time was lost.

After waving Bea off the following morning, it came back to her, and she drew it, the first of many times.

*

Something felt funny. What was that feeling? She stopped, touched her tummy. Strange noises coming from there. Hunger! She needed Doritos.

The corner shop was crammed with naughtiness. Rose wanted more than Doritos. She put a large bar of Dairy Milk, a bottle of Diet Coke, two packets of cheese and onion crisps and a large cheesy Doritos on the counter and listened as the register pinged.

'Sorry?' The woman looked grumpy. Unhappy. She was fat. Yeah, Rose could write about her. One of the kids on the farm would steal from her. Wendy, maybe.

Tilly would take the stolen sweets back. The grump would catch her doing it. Yeah! *Ping, ping* went the register.

'What?'

Oops, she must have said *ping, ping* out loud. She laughed. 'I thought that was in my head.'

'That's five pounds twenty.' The woman started bagging the goodies. She packed them so carefully! Neat and tidy, lifting the thin blue plastic carrier bag and dropping it again once filled to check she'd done a good job, and that the bag would hold. When Rose extended her hand to take it, the woman retreated, stared. The pause seemed interminable. 'That's mine.'

'And it's five pounds twenty.'

Oh. That's right. Money. She had to pay the grump for this bag. She wouldn't steal like Wendy had! She reached for the floral satchel she always used, but the long strap wasn't across her shoulder and the satchel wasn't banging at her hip like it always did. She must have left it somewhere.

'Oh no, I forgot my bag. I'll go get it. Can you keep those things till I get back?'

She sighed, the woman. Plonked the bag under the counter, picked up the magazine she'd been reading.

This place was soulless. Concrete boxes for houses growing out of the short shopping strip like straggly grey hair. Four wide lanes of road cut the area in half. But

Rose loved to wander, always had. She looked at the group of boys at the bus stop. Must have been around twelve. They were smoking. 'Shouldn't you boys be at school?'

The joker of the pack snarled at her: 'Shouldn't you be dead?'

The body count in her next book was mounting. Across the road was a large hotel, just as concretey and boxy as the houses surrounding it. A businessman in a suit, briefcase in hand, entered through the revolving door. *What boring conference are you attending?*

A young couple came out a few seconds later, holding hands. *I know what you've been up to.*

'Excuse me!' A car had stopped beside her, window zzing down. A young woman, around twenty-five perhaps, smiled.

'Are you lost?' Rose asked.

'I was going to ask you the same thing! Where you off to?'

'I'm . . .' This girl had groovy clothes. A floaty cream top, brown knee-high flat boots. She was so pretty. 'You don't need all the make-up! Why don't you try two days a week without lipstick to start, see how it goes, like they tell you to do with alcohol.'

'Okay!'

Her lips were so red. 'Oh! I need help. Can you help me?'

'Sure. Do you want me to drop you home? You know where you live?'

'No no. I mean yes. I do know that. But it's not that I need help with. Can you keep a secret?'

'I am a vault!' The girl twisted her fingers at her lips, as if locking them. She had the loveliest smile. 'Your smile would be so much nicer without the lipstick. Will you? Will you try without? Tomorrow? See how it feels. I bet you get even more compliments.'

'I will, if you tell me the secret.'

Oh. Oh, yes. The secret. 'It's . . . it's um. What's your name?'

'Sophie. Sophie Craig. What's your name?'

'Rose Price. I'm a writer!'

'Rose Price? Not the . . . Tilly? Rose Price! Oh wow. I LOVED your books as a kid. You want me to tell you a secret?'

'I'd love you to.'

'I still read them. The night before my Higher Exams, I read the one about Josie the cow over and over. How Tilly walked all night to put her in Farmer Greg's pasture. They calm me down, that one's my fave.'

'In real life, I ate Josie.' The girl went white and Rose felt bad for telling her the real-life version. 'I was so hungry.'

'Rose, I am such a fan. Let me take you home. I'll drop you off at your house.'

Rose had never been great with directions. Writers shouldn't be, she'd always told herself. Getting lost, wandering, that's where good stories came from.

'It's in Kelvindale?'

'Yes, yes, Kelvindale.'

'So, left at Hyndland Road? See up ahead – that's Hyndland Road. You recognise it?'

She did! 'Yes! Left here. Left again. See that wee lane past the ghost house?'

'Ghost house?'

'I always called it that. There are ghosts in there, don't you think? Loads of the things. Never saw anyone go in or out. Ghosts live there.'

'So right into this lane?'

'Yes. That's my house! Oh, my home!' She'd stopped at the gate. Rose opened the door, got out. She loved this place. Loved it! 'I wrote twenty-six books in there. Can you believe it?'

'I'd be inspired if I lived here too.' The girl was getting out as well.

Was she wanting a cup of tea?

'I would love a cup of tea.'

As usual, the whitewashed gate was locked. Rose reached for her keys. 'Damn! My bag. I wonder if I left it in the house.'

The kind girl jumped the gate into Rose's stone-paved courtyard and opened it to let Rose in. The flowers were all gone! Just a couple of sad-looking potted shrubs. Someone had ruined her garden.

They looked through the kitchen window together. Perhaps she'd left the bag on the kitchen table. That wasn't her kitchen table. Hers was old-fashioned, country-kitchen style, big enough to lay out her drawing pads and her paints. This table was white and new. Where was her kitchen table?

Rose wasn't sure what happened in the minutes after that. She was sitting on the ground now. The girl with the make-up was phoning someone.

'Who are you phoning?'

'It's okay. I'm just trying to find out where your bag is.'

'I left the Doritos at the shop.' The girl's lipstick was so red. 'Oh! Call the police! Please, call the police! I live in Dear Green Care Home. People are being killed there. Please, will you call the police?'

The girl had stopped talking on the phone, was putting the handset back in her bag. 'I have. I have called the police. They've been looking for you, Rose. They'll be here in a minute. It's okay, it's okay.'

Rose nodded sadly. Dear Green. The name had seemed lovely when Chris first mentioned it. Dear Green. She'd thought about using it in her next book.

'While we wait, tell me about your writing. Where do you get your ideas from?'

She could talk about writing for ever! It felt so good. On the garden furniture someone had put in the barren courtyard, she told her all about Vernon. How she'd come to life after he died, not that he was a bad man, not that motherhood wasn't rewarding. She even changed her surname back to Price again. She was Rose Price, not Rose Wife. How she blossomed after all that was dusted and done.

'You mean done and dusted?'

'I prefer dusted and done.'

She talked about the book festivals she'd attended – in Berlin, Chicago, Brisbane. She talked about the little girls she met at schools, eyes wide open with greedy pleasure as she read from her books. She talked about Tilly, who was the wee girl she'd failed to be.

She'd been talking a while before she realised two police officers were standing in the courtyard listening to her stories. One looked familiar, a friend of Chris's perhaps. The other looked about fifteen and was grumpy with her. 'Where's your tag, Rose?'

'My what?'

'Never mind. I hear you were trying to get help? What do you need help with exactly?'

She could do with a lot of help! She wanted to go to for a mooch in town and she could do with a lift.

She was hungry and would love a roll and sausage. She needed plants, plants, as someone had taken them all.

'Are you police officers?'

The older, kinder one, nodded.

'Well, someone has stolen my plants.'

CHAPTER TWENTY-ONE

I wonder what I'd have written in my advanced care planning statement. Let me think. I would have wanted to die at home, probably, in the house I shared with Mum. A few weeks ago, I'd have asked that she be by my side. I'd have asked her to pretend that heaven exists and to list all the fab things about it in that deep serious voice of hers. With Mum gone, I'd have asked for Paul. I'd have liked him to sit on the bed and hold my hand. No! I'd want him to stand by the bed and— No! He should sit in a chair and read, no sing, no, no, talk to me, yeah, talk, about that drama class we did when we were teenagers and how I was too sullen to pretend to be anything other than sullen. And about all those movies we watched together, dissecting them after and him saying, 'You're wrong about the turning point, Catherine, wrong!' And about how I secretly studied hard for my Highers behind my friends' backs – late into the night in his bedroom or in mine – and how I hid my results from Gina and Co. 'cause As were way uncool and how I worried about showing them to Mum 'cause she'd want me to do law or something and about how proud I was when I did show her. I reckon I'd have asked Paul to be mushy. I'd have wanted him to tell me he loves me and that I'm beautiful. I'd have wanted him to tell me about the flat we'd have lived in together and the places we'd have travelled to. I'd have wanted to continue what we started – another kiss but no tongues, 'cause mine'd probably taste like death.

I wonder what music I would have wanted. Would I have asked for music? I don't know. My fads were short lived.

If I wrote the statement more than a month ago, I'd definitely have said I wanted to die before getting old and smelly and boring and slow and embarrassing. I'd have asked for it to be quick and painless and without fear and in my sleep and I'd have absolutely insisted on having a decent but appropriate outfit on, like my cute stripy PJ bottoms and a fresh sleeveless white T-shirt for instance (similar to Mum's!). I'd have asked Paul to make sure my mouth didn't drool during and droop after and that someone closed my eyes immediately if they stayed open and that if they were to post RIP photos about me online or put some up at the service, they should be chosen from the profile pic folder on my Facebook page 'cause they are all fucking stunning. I would not have asked for this.

When I woke, it took me a while to understand where I was. The bed was comfortable, the room quiet and softly lit. For a moment, I thought I was at home, but then a landscape painting unblurred a bit and after that a handrail or two as well and I wondered if I'd fallen asleep in Mum's room in Dear Green, but then I remembered that Mum had gone already and that heavy feeling happened, that wave of hot leaden sorrow that had come and gone since she died, and then I realised I had no reason to be there. When I tried to sit up I remembered the last thing that happened before waking here – Chris's arms reaching out, hitting me – and I knew I was in Room 7.

Gina's mate from London had a date rape experience once and for a while after we all remembered to be careful with our drinks. Her name was Kate. Gina's half-brother found her lying in the car park outside the bar full of Ketamine and some guy's sperm. Apparently after, she said the worst thing was not being able to remember anything about it, and I always thought that was wacko – who'd want to remember being sexually assaulted? I suppose they'd given me something similar. Everything was wonky. I couldn't move. I wanted to kick the restraints off and run but I couldn't do either of those things. I wanted to forget this already.

I wasn't being raped; not yet, anyway. I was alone in the room. I wondered if that's what they were going to do. Maybe not. Maybe they wouldn't touch me. Maybe they'd just watch me die. I shut my eyes and opened them again, unsure why I could move my eyelids but nothing else. When they came in – the people who drove here in the middle of the night to stand, in all sorts of shoes, around my bed – I could close my eyes and pretend they weren't there at all. Perhaps this wouldn't be too hard. As long as they didn't need to see my fear, or the reflection in my eyes. As long as they didn't need to touch me.

It was a bland stage. Just me on the trolley bed, Velcro bands stretching across legs, torso, shoulders. The door was shut and I could hear footsteps and faint male chatter. Oh, I could try and yell! Why hadn't I thought of that? To yell, my mouth needed to be open, but I couldn't work out how to make that happen. I studied my blinking for a minute or two – my eyelids shut, and then they opened. I tried to pinpoint how I had managed to make this happen in order to transfer the skills to my mouth. No. I couldn't do it.

The painting opposite me was moving. A block of green at the bottom swayed beneath a mess of colour above. I shut my eyes again. Maybe I could yell without my mouth being open. Or just talk even. Just a sound, any sound. *Nup*. Oh that painting had to stop moving! Those noises had to stop noising... tappety, tappety tap-tap-tap, in time with the moving green on the wall.

Bang. The space beside the painting changed. A door, open now, some people coming in, closing it again. If

I could blink, surely I could yell, please, mouth, do as you're told and yell! Maybe Nurse Gabriella was here and would hear me, come to my rescue. If not her, who? Paul was to come with food. That's right. At eight. Was it after eight? No idea. If he'd gone to my house, he might have assumed I'd forgotten, or gone out, or fallen into a deep sleep. He probably left a message or two, then went home to study. I'd never been a very reliable friend with Paul – always late (6. Catherine's timekeeping) or rescheduling (7. Catherine's poor organisational skills) or forgetting (8. Catherine's absent-mindedness). No, Paul wouldn't rescue me, and there was no one else.

There were three men in the room. No, four. No, three. There were men in the room.

No, one was a woman. Short, rotund, a hundred times grotesque. Harriet. The others were men, though.

'Just Rose to get down,' Harriet said, I think. 'Wondering actually, can I make myself some toast later?'

'Yes, that's okay,' someone said. 'I disabled the alarm as usual, so keep a keen nose, won't you.'

From Harriet again, 'Yes, sir; buzz me when it's break time and I'll get the kettle on. I've prepared the buffet. And I'll be in the office all night. Right you are.'

*

I guess most film sets are bland before the staging. The

men had so much to do! The laptop monitor was placed on the bedside table and turned on, camera pointing at me. If I turned my eyeballs, I could see myself on the screen, right in the centre, my swirling other self at centre stage, a counter at the bottom indicating that viewers were already tuning in.

'Fifty-five in two minutes!' one of the men said. Chris, that was Chris. He was smartly dressed for tonight's show. He was excited. 'Fifty-six, fifty-seven. fifty-eight! Check it out!'

The sound had to be checked. 'Testing, testing,' one of the other men said, then he moved a piece of equipment and said it again. Jimmy, that was Jimmy. Hey there, Jimmy. He had a spliff in his mouth, sucked in a huge mouthful, blew it in my face, said, 'It's good to giggle.'

'Sixty hits, and we've not even prepared her! Imagine after make-up and wardrobe.' The man who said this was Marcus Baird. 'How many tickets sold?' Marcus was obviously the business head.

'Eleven at three hundred, four at four. And Mr F has booked some private time for after.' Chris was adding up the takings on paper as he spoke.

'How much?'

'Two thousand for an hour. JX has enquired too. Might get a few privates depending on time. Maybe offer half an hour at twelve hundred?'

Chris, Marcus and Jimmy sat down for a meeting, at least that's what it looked like. There was much to discuss before Action. Marcus wanted to clarify that, like the last one, I was an emergency measure only, that this site was not about torture or killing, that this kind of thing had never been his intention. Chris clarified that this and the last one were one-offs, that they had no choice, but that it would have been madness not to capitalise on a tricky and dangerous situation. Marcus wanted to know what would happen with the actor afterwards. Chris calmed him, he had it all sorted.

I didn't take in much else. Something about payment for Harriet, something about security and the anonymity of the viewers, something about how long the drug would work, how best to get the job done. 'A gentle death,' Chris decided, like with the last one. 'As you said, this isn't about torture. And she's so beautiful and innocent. Gentle, yeah, gentle.'

Boxes of tissues were placed about the room and the pictures on the wall were covered over with cloth. Then Chris began to clean up the actor. That was me, by the way.

I've panicked in the past. When I lost all my friends at T in the Park music festival, for example, and when I thought I was pregnant that time. Looking back, I didn't mind the combination of fear and helplessness, because it was swiftly followed by adrenaline and solutions. In this instance, adrenaline would not rescue me because there were no solutions. I tried Mum's mantra 'Just don't think about it'. But three men had drugged me and one was now cleansing my face with wipes. They were going to kill me. How could I not think about this?

I tried another strategy – the 'other me' one I talked about so naively earlier on. Why think about difficult things, why plan for them, when another me altogether will be the one to deal with them? This me, the one lying paralysed and tied on a table, was the only me available. I had no choice but to worry about this.

The worry filled me, knocked at me from the inside.

Mum was here, I thought. She'd had this man cleanse her face and pull her trousers off and put a silver nightie on. She'd had a grotesque face breathe on her as he applied concealer, foundation, lipstick, liner, blusher, mascara.

He held his tongue between his teeth as he worked, concentrating. She'd probably, hopefully, been unconscious while her hair was brushed carefully, almost lovingly, and placed about the pillow. Marcus intermittently checked how it looked on the laptop screen. And it was looking pretty good, just a few tweaks: less on the cheeks, move the strap off the shoulder a little, that's it, no a bit less, that's it, yes! Seventy-three hits already, and no wonder because 'This is looking lovely!'

Chris and Jimmy left the room to spruce themselves

up and Marcus sat on the bed. 'I'm sorry about this, Catherine.' He kissed me on the forehead. 'Don't be scared, we're not going to hurt you.' He kissed my lips. (*Yell, mouth, yell!*) 'You're so pretty when you're still.' He pricked my arm, and placed a tube in it. My blood began to drain into a bottle. So this is how I'd die, I'd be emptied into bottles, litre by litre. Drip, drip, drip; tick, tick, tick, 109, 110.

'Ten minutes till curtains!' That was Chris back again. He'd put some make-up on too, by the looks.

'Ten minutes, Catherine,' Marcus smiled at me. 'You're gonna be great.'

Chris opened a bottle of champagne as Gavin wheeled his catatonic wife into the room. He poured them all a drink. 'They'll arrive soon. We ready?'

'We're ready!'

Clink!

*

I closed my eyes and thought about the list I'd left on the coffee table back home. I hadn't finished writing it yet. It was going to be very long because there were hundreds of things I wanted to do. While a few weeks ago I had no hopes and no dreams, now I had millions. I think I might have done a lot of the things on the list. I would have fallen in love. It would have been with Paul.

I couldn't help but smile at this thought and decided I'd lie there and continue thinking it for the rest of my life. Paul and I are kissing, mmm.

Remember me, won't you, because you won't be hearing from me again. I'm twenty-three, female, healthy. I have blonde hair and blue eyes. I'm slim, athletic and cute as a button.

Dammit.

If you want to check out what happened to me, click <u>here</u>.

CHAPTER TWENTY-TWO

AGE 82

Maybe it was kind of like tinnitus, a buzzing or humming not just in your ear but in your entire head and it makes the world sinister.

Or maybe it was like a series of dreams, bad ones mostly.

Oh fuck it, Rose would never be able to describe it. She scrunched another page of crappy idiotic writing, lifted her bedside cabinet to the side so it rested at an angle against the bed, and removed two of the boxes of matches taped underneath. Twenty-seven boxes she'd found since she moved here, that's more than one a month. A message, perhaps, but she didn't understand it. Ah, the other thing taped there was a phone! Catherine had given it to her. Press 1 for Catherine. 2 for 999. She untaped the phone and put it and one box of matches in the pouch of her koala onesie.

One of the perks of being locked in this room was that she could strike matches and burn her shit pieces of writing without being reprimanded like a schoolgirl.

She loved burning shit writing. She shook the remaining ashes of her latest effort into the bin.

A maze, yes, that's what it was like. Had she just thought of that now? Clever! She'd been wandering around a God almighty maze, neat trimmed hedges enticing her this way, that, until – inevitably – she found herself at the hedge that had been carved out as a lion, or something, and knew she had been there before, that in fact she had got nowhere, just round and round and round again.

Her daughter should come and help her out. Two, she had two daughters. Why were they not hollering from the exit – This way, Mum! Follow my voice.

The dumpy care assistant came in to her room, just like that, without even knocking. The people here were ruder than anyone she'd ever known. She sniffed the smoky air, 'Have you stolen matches from the kitchen again?'

Rose handed Harriet a pack of matches, smiling on the inside, because there was another in her pouch and twenty-five taped to the bottom of her bedside cabinet.

'Now, bedtime!'

'I'm not tired.'

'Yes you are.'

'I know when I'm tired and I'm telling you I'm not.'

'Lie down in bed, Rose, let's not have any trouble tonight.'

'There won't be any trouble. I'm just not tired.'

'Good! Lie down now. Bed.'

Harriet pulled the sheets back and now had a firm hold on Rose's arm.

'You're hurting me.'

'No, I'm not.'

If anything, the hold increased in severity. A pinch, Rose would call that a definite pinch.

'You're pinching me. Don't push me down!'

'I'm not pushing. Now, now, just on the mattress, nice and comfy, that's it. Open your mouth.'

'What is that?'

'Your pill.'

'What pill?'

'The one you need to take. There. Now some water, and swallow, that's it.'

Rose pretended to swallow, and manoeuvred her tongue to lodge the pill underneath it. 'Now get out of my room, you ugly, ugly woman.'

*

AGE 10

The problem was this: Rose was a city girl. Her chores growing up had been city chores. She was not good at milking cows and wading through mud and eating her favourite cow for lunch. She was not good at lighting fires.

She'd been trying a while now, but there were no twigs here and she had looked everywhere. Her dad's words echoed through her head as she hunted for kindling. You're a selfish girl, Rose Price. She would prove him wrong. If Margie was too weak to get to the doctor, she would get the doctor to come here. First, she had to make the fire.

There was always something other-worldly about Margie, as if she knew from infancy that she would be different, sickly, dependent, and somehow this impressed a look of composure and great dignity on her face. She never complained, she never cried. Like Beth out of *Little Women*. No, not Beth! Beth died. Margie would be fine. Rose just needed to get kindling.

But there was no kindling. Rose stamped her foot in frustration. She had to hurry! There was no time to look for twigs. She grabbed what she could find – a book from the shelf, pulled the colourful pages out, scrunched them into balls. No, one book was not enough. She grabbed another and another and another, all thirty of them, pulling the pages out in a fury, piling them on the ground before her, topping them with the hard backs now emptied of their silly stories and drawings. Now, city girl or not, that was a decent looking bonfire. All she needed was a box of matches.

*

AGE 82

Bzzz. Bzzz. The noise made Rose jump back from the door she must have been trying to open. Someone had pressed the buzzer in their room. It bzzz'd into the office. She heard frumpy footsteps on office floor. 'Yes, sir, of course,' Harriet's formal tone matched her words. 'That's fine, all ready in five minutes.'

Oh God, that's right, Rose remembered! She'd heard this exact sequence before. She knew what was going to come next.

Frumpy footsteps over hall, into dining room, light switched on, kettle switched on, footsteps from kitchen to dining room, trays being placed on table, and again, cling film being removed from tray, tray, tray, footsteps dining room to kitchen, kettle hissing, and back, three corks taking turns to squeak their way to freedom, kitchen, back, cups and glasses and more glasses on table, pause. And then they came, just as they did the other times. The night Bea died. Emma, Jason. A flock of whispering footsteps now as before, moving from Room 7 towards the dining room until someone closed the door and it was silent.

Oh, it all made sense, and she remembered, and she understood, and how she wished she didn't but she did.

She knew she must have missed many of these little gatherings, but she'd been in her room listening to this sequence three times, maybe more. They'd be in the dining room, door shut, for about half an hour, but someone would go and check Room 7 every ten minutes. So Rose had nine minutes now. All the time in the world.

*

She put her hand in the pouch of her koala onesie. Ha. Matches, phone. She lit the fire she'd built. Hairpin in hand, she picked her lock open, closed her door, and ran as fast as she could to Room 7. To her surprise, they hadn't locked it. A cocky bunch, this lot. She opened the door, pulled the needle from Catherine's arm, pushed the brake levers on the wheels of the bed, and – using all her strength – pushed the bed out of the room, and down the hall to the front door. They were still in the dining room, chattering away.

*

Out the door, down the ramp, across the gravel, over wet bumpy grass. This was difficult, but she had to keep going. But she couldn't. She had to rest. She stopped, caught her breath, took out the phone and pressed 2.

'This is Nurse Gabriella Nelson. I'm ringing to report a fire at Dear Green Care Home in Clydebank.'

Then she pushed and pushed until they got to the tree, turning to watch her prison cell brighten, smoke leaking from its windows. The watchers hadn't come outside. They were still in the dining room; they may not have even smelt the smoke yet when the fire engines arrived.

A weak finger reached for her hand. Catherine. Rose bent over the trolley, placed her forehead against Catherine's, and sang.

Her voice could not drown out the noises in the distance. Sirens. The skid of car tyres. A voice on loudspeaker saying, 'Please gather in the rose garden! Please do not leave the grounds!' Hoses. Shouting. Sirens: ambulance, police. Shouting. Silence.

Rose stopped singing.

The girl had so little life left in her, and she used all of it to smile at Rose and say: 'You stayed with me, Ro-Ro, you stayed.'

Rose smiled at this perfect girl. As kind and as lovable as her little sister, but not her little sister. Oh, Catherine. 'I did! I stayed with you. I stayed with you, angel.'

Acknowledgements

I'd like to thank my Dad, who died of a brain tumour, and his Mum, who suffered from dementia.

A big 'ta' to Sergio Casci, Liz Hopkin, Doug Johnstone and Luca Veste who read early drafts for me and gave honest and helpful feedback.

Thanks to my agent, Philip Patterson at Marjacq Scripts, for reading, re-reading, and keeping me motivated.

And to the fabulous folk at Faber, especially Sarah Savitt, Katherine Armstrong, Sophie Portas and Trevor Horwood.

Q&A with Helen FitzGerald

The two main characters in THE EXIT have a big age gap: Catherine is 23 and Rose is 82. Did you find it easier to capture the voice of someone younger than you, or older, or does the age of the characters not matter in this way when you're writing fiction?

I deliberately didn't want to be ageist. I just wanted to think of Catherine and Rose as people, real women, and I hope the authenticity of voice sprang from that. I suppose I did draw on my daughter (17) who, like Catherine, is wondering what she wants to do with her life and taking a lot of selfies; and on Mum (80), who grew up on a dairy farm and loves to write and draw. I'm very close to both of them, and this helped me feel close to Rose and Catherine.

Several of the characters in THE EXIT turn out to have been harbouring major secrets. Do you think most people are hiding something from the world?

I live in an area lined with red sandstone terraces and I'm

always imagining the secrets that might be kept inside the identical houses – (A cross-dresser? An adulterer? A domestic abuser? A cocaine addict?) So yes, I do think everyone has a story, but most people find it impossible to keep a secret to themselves. They have to tell someone.

As well as writing, you work as a social worker for people on parole. How does this affect your writing?

The essential skills for both jobs are the same: empathy and nosiness. I don't think the job affects my writing; it's just that they're both suited to me as a person. As a social worker and as a writer I deal with people in crisis. In both jobs I get to know the perpetrator, I gather information, and I assess the risks. In both I hold the belief that ordinary people can do bad things.

THE EXIT is set in a care home and some of the characters are facing the prospect of death. Did writing the book make you think about death and end-of-life care (for example the debate around euthanasia) differently?

My Dad died a few months before I started writing *The Exit*. I spent two months with him as a brain tumour gradually eroded his faculties. I googled The Brain

Hospice Timeline endlessly, wondering what stage he was at, how long he had left. I was with him when a nurse went over his end of life choices (Advanced Care Planning Statement). She asked him bizarre questions that I couldn't have answered either ('If you couldn't walk, would you want to live?' My Dad said: 'Well I'd be in a very bad mood'). End of Life care was very much on my mind. I've since watched films like *Amour*, almost obsessed with the euthanasia debate. But I don't know what I think, or what I'd want. It's not till it happens to you, or someone you love, that you realise how complex and profound a question it really is.

Rose is slipping into dementia, which means that no one believes her when she insists that there is a dark secret at the heart of her care home. How did you do your research on dementia? Was it more disturbing in some ways to write about dementia than something you might find more often in a crime novel, for example murder?

My grandmother died with dementia. I remember visiting her at Nazareth House in Melbourne as a daft eighteen-year-old, feeling nervous and uncomfortable. After a nurse left the room, she said: 'That woman is trying to kill me!' I didn't know what to say, and didn't

301

say anything; I dismissed it. But what if she was telling the truth?

Before writing this book, I talked to people who'd been affected by dementia. I read a lot of articles and blogs by dementia patients and carers. It's such a difficult illness, one a third of us will face in later years. Yes, I found it more disturbing than writing about a murder.

In your two most recent novels – THE EXIT and THE CRY – you've explored the dark side of social media: rumours, bullying, criminal underworlds . . . How do you feel about Facebook and Twitter? Have you experienced their dark sides?

My husband wrote a film called *The Caller*, and was in Puerto Rico while it was being filmed. A Facebook friend of mine also happened to be a fan of Stephen Moyer (Vampire Bill in *True Blood*) who was the lead in the film. I was chatting to my husband online, and he said Stephen Moyer had told him he was reading my book (*The Donor*) in bed. Minutes later, I was chatting to my friend on Facebook, and I mentioned it. Two hours later, my husband called to say that Stephen Moyer was worried because a blogger had written a story about what he was reading in bed! Oops, my bad.

I love and hate the internet. I love the online crime-writing community, and I need the camaraderie and banter. But I often feel a sick sense of shame when I over-share, and I have had nasty comments and veiled threats from someone in the past. It takes a while to learn the rules: don't overshare, don't tweet drunk, and remember it's public, and it's permanent.

Catherine has a good relationship with her mother in the novel, but they both hide things from each other. You often tackle taboos in your fiction and I wondered – does your mother read your books?

Mum is a retired literature teacher, and a wonderful writer. When I eventually emailed her my first book, terrified about her reaction to the sweary words and sex scenes, I waited nervously for a week before asking her if she'd read it yet. It hadn't arrived. God or someone had intervened. I sent it again with an email asking her not to read page 1, page 33, page 57–59 (etc. etc.). She called back three hours later having read all of it. She said she wished she hadn't read the pages listed above, but was otherwise very proud. Since then, she's been one of the first to read all of my drafts.

You're married to a screenwriter. What are the differences between writing fiction and writing screenplays? Do you help each other with writing and editing?

As a novelist, you are the writer, the producer, the director, and the performer. You have to decide on everything, you fill in the blanks. My husband says he has staff for all that boring stuff! I tried screenwriting before novel-writing, and it was a great training ground for me, but I find writing books much easier. It comes more naturally to me.

I'm sitting in bed writing the answers to these questions. An hour ago I was staring at the screen, unable to think of a thing to say. I messaged my husband on Facebook (he was watching TV downstairs) and asked him if he wanted to come up and help me. A minute later he appeared at the door, 'Yay! A job!' He helps me with absolutely everything.

Also by Helen FitzGerald

ff

THE CRY

He's gone.

And telling the truth won't bring him back . . .

When a baby goes missing on a lonely roadside in
Australia, it sets off a police investigation that
will become a media sensation and dinner-table
talk across the world.

Lies, rumours and guilt snowball, causing the parents,
Joanna and Alistair, to slowly turn against each other.

Finally Joanna starts thinking the unthinkable: could
the truth be even more terrible than she suspected?
And what will it take to make things right?

The Cry is a dark psychological thriller with a gripping
moral dilemma at its heart and characters who will
keep you guessing on every page.

'Exceptional . . . this powerful noir tale is by turns
devastating and uplifting.' **Chris Ewan**,
Number One bestselling author of *Safe House*

ff

THE DONOR

Two daughters. One impossible choice.

Just after her sixteenth birthday, Will's daughter Georgie
suffers kidney failure. She needs a transplant but her
type is rare. Will, a single dad who's given up everything
to raise his twin daughters, offers to be a donor.

Then his other daughter, Katy, gets sick. She's just
as precious, her kidney type just as rare. Time is
critical, and Will has to make a decision.

Should he try to buy a kidney? Should he save just one
child – if so, which one? Should he sacrifice himself?
Or is there a fourth solution, one so terrible it has
never even crossed his mind?

'Everybody should read everything that Helen FitzGerald
has written. She is dark, clever, highly inventive.'
Lovereading.co.uk Great Reads Pick

ff

DEAD LOVELY

What happens when your best friend gets what you've always wanted?

Krissie and Sarah – best friends for years – have always wanted different things from life. Krissie has no desire to settle down, whereas Sarah married a doctor in her early twenties and is dying to start a family. So when Krissie becomes pregnant after a fling and Sarah can't seem to conceive, things get a little tense.

Krissie and Sarah decide to go on holiday along with Sarah's husband in the hope of getting their friendship back on track. But what starts as a much-needed break soon becomes a nightmare of sexual tension, murder and mayhem . . .

'Outrageous, clever, funny, poignant. Helen FitzGerald really is one to watch.' **Mo Hayder**

'A gripping, addictive psycho-thriller.' *Big Issue*

'Gloriously black comedy.' *Herald*

ff

MY LAST CONFESSION

A naïve parole officer in her first month on the job. An extremely good-looking convicted murderer. What could go wrong?

These are some of Krissie's tips for fellow parole officers:

Don't smuggle heroin into prison.

Don't drink vodka to relieve stress.

Don't French-kiss a colleague to make your boyfriend jealous.

If only she'd taken her own advice . . .

When she starts the job, Krissie is happy and in love. Then she meets convicted murderer Jeremy, and begins to believe he may be innocent. Her growing obsession with his case threatens to jeopardise everything – her job, her relationship and her life.

'Thinking woman's noir.' *Sunday Telegraph*

'Cool, classy, sexy.' *Daily Mirror*

'Satisfyingly shocking.' *Big Issue*